Roost - Text copyright © Emmy Ellis 2025
Cover Art by Emmy Ellis @ studioenp.com © 2025

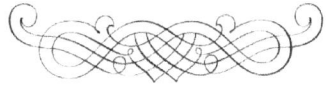

All Rights Reserved

Roost is a work of fiction. All characters, places, and events are from the author's imagination. Any resemblance to persons, living or dead, events or places is purely coincidental.

The author respectfully recognises the use of any and all trademarks.

With the exception of quotes used in reviews, this book may not be reproduced or used in whole or in part by any means existing without written permission from the author.

Warning: The unauthorised reproduction or distribution of this copyrighted work is illegal. No part of this book may be scanned, uploaded, or distributed via the Internet or any other means, electronic or print, without the author's written permission. The author does not give permission for any part of this book to be used in AI.

Published by Five Pyramids Press, Suite 1a 34 West Street,
Retford, England, DN22 6ES
ISBN: 9798283004228

ROOST

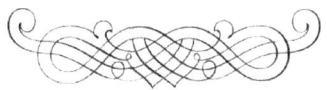

Emmy Ellis

Prologue

<u>*Saturday 27th July 2024*</u>

All day I've been tempted to open the bag and look inside, but what's the point when I won't even see anything worth seeing? Maybe it was the urge to make sure the contents are really in there. Like, I did <u>it</u>

but I just needed to make sure. Every time I went down there today I was tempted, and I had to tell myself off for being so stupid. Of course it's in the bag. I helped put it there. I saw it.

Because we were so busy yesterday and I was tired, I ended up staying over, which went against what we'd planned. All I wanted to do was go home and curl up in my own bed, but seriously, I was so knackered emotionally. I did a bad thing, and even though I planned it, the reality hit me pretty hard. Harder than I imagined it would.

I'm not quite sure how to feel about who I am now. Have I become something? Someone new? Someone with a label? I suppose I have, although it isn't a label I'll be telling anyone about.

I woke up during the night after a nasty dream, demons chasing me, or maybe that's my conscience playing tricks—and it'd serve me right. I knew I was capable of doing whatever it took to get what I wanted, I just didn't think I'd go as far as I did.

People won't look at me the same if this ever gets out.

No use crying over spilt milk. It's time to put the other things into action. Earn the money so I can have a better life. Buy a house. Move away from the council estate. I bet if Mum's watching from up there she won't be smiling. She'll be ashamed of me. But I've done it now, there's no turning the clock back, so it's walk forward or give up, and I'm fucked if I'll give up. Not now.

Chapter One

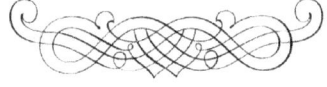

The men came and went with their wallets considerably depleted once they'd shut the front door and got in their vehicles. It was always the same, every night without fail. Mum made a packet out of them by spreading her legs, probably doing other stuff, too, and it wouldn't be so bad if Miranda didn't have to hear it all going on. The walls were thin, Mum's

headboard whacked into the one between their bedrooms, so Miranda locked herself away in the kitchen at the back of the house every evening. It was all right, there was a little telly on the sideboard if she fancied watching it or she needed to deaden the noise, but she had homework to do anyway.

Sometimes, Miranda played a game where she pretended this wasn't her life. In her daydreams she had a proper mum and dad who were still a couple, and they went out on dates even though they'd been together for years. Mum was a secretary not a slapper, and none of the neighbours ever gave them filthy looks when they left the house.

Her real life was far from that, though.

Mum never had a night off. She said there was too much money to be made and too many other women who would take her place if she wasn't available. Apparently, it was a small world, the one Mum inhabited, and word soon got round if someone wasn't up to par. Anyway, she couldn't afford not to work, what with being a single parent. She said that a lot, maybe to let Miranda know it hadn't been Mum's fault that her father wasn't around, or maybe she was proud of coping by herself, not that Miranda would ever know it. Mum tended to hide a lot of her true feelings when it came to private stuff, but she was happy enough to voice them if it meant telling Miranda off or ordering her about.

Her mother was a bitch.

Miranda often wondered where her dad was—who he was—and whether, if she ever found him, he'd want her in his life. She'd learned not to bring him up with her mum, who said she didn't even know who he was. If Mum had been doing what she did now to make money back then, it was obvious why. Six different men a night, none of them wearing condoms. Take your pick who Daddy is, darling.

Footsteps on the stairs. Mr Swanson, one of the customers, must be leaving. Miranda jumped when the kitchen door opened. Oh God, he stood there staring at her, smiling this really weird smile. She wasn't sure whether to smile back or not just in case it encouraged him. She needn't have worried, because he walked over to the sink and took a glass from the cupboard, filling it with water and drinking it down in three swallows. Then he rinsed the glass and popped it on the draining board to dry, staring at his reflection in the window. He had one of those strange thick moustaches that reminded her of broom bristles. It was brown at the roots and ginger on the ends. The ginger matched his hair, but his eyelashes behind the lenses of his black glasses were almost white, as were his eyebrows. He had loads of freckles on really pale skin. There was a girl at school who was the same, ginger and pale.

He never usually came into the kitchen like this, so Miranda felt uneasy. Had he only popped in for water? No, he looked like he was about to say something. She wished he'd just go, because having a chat with Mr Swanson wasn't high on her to-do list. He gave her the creeps.

He smiled the smile of someone who was uncertain as to what response he'd receive. "Err, your mother said you need to go upstairs."

Miranda lowered her pen to lay it in the spine crease of her open textbook. She stood on wobbly legs — something was going on, and it didn't sit right with her. What if Mr Swanson had hurt Mum? Miranda couldn't think of any other reason why she'd need to go up there. Mum always wanted her to stay away when she was working. Nevertheless, Miranda scooted past him to run upstairs to her mother's bedroom, his footsteps following her all the way in threatening thuds. Why did he have to come up, too? Why didn't he just fuck off home?

Shit, is he going to hurt me?

Miranda burst into the bedroom, out of breath, her chest tight with her building anxiety. It was all very well hating your mother, and she really did, but it was another thing altogether to imagine her dead and you having to tell the police that some pervert had done it. But Mum stood by the window, completely unharmed in her red bra and knickers and those black stockings she loved so much. She bought about fifteen packets a week, all with the seam up the back, and she'd perfected the art of putting them on so those seams were perfectly straight. She held a bundle of white lace, which was probably one of her other lingerie sets; she generally changed outfits between customers after a quick wash at the bathroom sink. They didn't have a shower, but it was something Mum was desperate to get once she'd saved up enough money.

"Put this on." Mum held the lace out towards Miranda. Her eyes had that look that warned Miranda not to play her up, to just do as she was told like a good girl.

Miranda's stomach rolled over, and confusion clouded her head for a moment. Put it on? What? She was so conscious of Mr Swanson lurking nearby that the need to do a wee came on really strong.

"W…what for?"

Mum smiled, a shark about to attack if she so much as got a sniff of blood, but Miranda wasn't bleeding, not yet.

"It's time for you to start work," Mum explained.

Miranda went to step backwards, onto the landing, but bumped into Mr Swanson, the heat of his front on her back churning her stomach. He gripped the tops of her arms from behind, held her tighter than she thought he should, digging his fingertips in hard enough to leave bruises. Her heart raced as she thought about what 'start work' meant. Mum had said a few times she ought to get Miranda on the game, but she'd always laughed when she'd said it, so Miranda had thought she was joking.

She clearly wasn't.

Tears burned so harshly, emotion clogging her throat. She was trapped between her mother and a customer, no chance of getting away from either of them, because if she made a run for it, one of them would catch her.

Mum came closer with the lace. It still had a tag dangling off it, so she must have bought a new one. That was something, at least Miranda didn't have to wear Mum's castoffs, but she wished she didn't have to wear anything like that at all. And when had it been bought? Likely while Miranda had sat in class at school, completely oblivious that her mother had decided it was time for her to lose her virginity.

"He'll be gentle for your first time," Mum said.

Oh God, did she mean Mr Swanson? He didn't feel gentle. He squeezed her arms harder. His hot breath warmed her ear and neck where he'd lowered his head. Was he sniffing *her? He licked a wet stripe up her cheek, and Miranda shuddered. Why did Mum choose to do this every night? Did she actually like people slobbering all over her? Or had she been doing it for so long that she'd got used to it now and it was like any other job, something you did just to make money.*

Mum laughed. "You'll get used to it."

Had she read Miranda's mind?

Miranda tried to get away from him, squirming and wrenching her arms, but he held her too tightly. He tutted a lot every time she tried to shrug him off, the burn of shame prickling her cheeks. She kicked back at his shin, but her bare foot did sod all. The urge to run took over her, but he shoved her, propelling her towards the bed. Her knees hit the edge of the mattress, and she fell forward, him landing on top of her, knocking the wind out of her lungs. With her face squashed into the quilt she couldn't breathe, and panic reared its ugly head.

"You promised to be gentle with her," Mum said.

The pressure lifted with Mr Swanson rolling off to lie next to Miranda who moved her head to the side to take in big gasps of air. She stared directly at him, hating his face, his hair, is slack mouth, everything about him. He seemed puzzled as to why she didn't want to do this—didn't he realise he was old *and repulsive? Had Mum told him lies? Did he think Miranda was up for it? She'd known her mother wasn't the normal sort, but she'd never thought this would happen.*

She never thought she'd be sold off.

"If you work for me, then I'll tell you who your daddy is," Mum said.

Hope sprang up. If Mum did that, then Miranda could go to him. She could tell him about her shitty life and how she'd been treated.

Would he care? Would he keep her safe?

Miranda closed her eyes and let Mr Swanson do whatever he wanted.

Chapter Two

In a black dress, a red bolero jacket, and high heels, Miranda Stevens, who now went by the name of Pearl, sat in the back of the car with her boss, Jet Proust, leader of the Proust Estate. They were on their way to an art exhibition where Jet would meet with a drug supplier—the kind of meeting that looked innocent but was far from it.

A quiet little chat. Coy giggles while drinking champagne. All a cover for what was really going on.

Jet had been in talks with this particular dealer for weeks. So far the business had been conducted on the phone, Jet asking him questions to see whether his answers matched what her men had found out about him. Andre Alexander was from Italy but had resided in the UK for a few years. He was in his twenties, lived in a large four-storey Victorian house, and drove around in an expensive car. He said he'd stopped doing face-to-face meetings because his reputation preceded him, but Jet wasn't having any of that. She'd never rely on a man's—or woman's— word over the phone. She liked to see their expressions to check whether they were lying or insincere, and calling her bluff wasn't advised.

Pearl had done this sort of thing with her before. Two elegant-looking women were less likely to be suspected of drug dealing than if Jet had sent a couple of her men to the meeting, and the venue was hardly a place where the buying and selling of drugs was usually discussed. They'd be in and out within an hour, so Jet had said, and then they'd go to the Montreal for dinner.

Pearl's stomach rumbled. She hadn't eaten since breakfast.

"Keep your eye on Andre for me when we're speaking," Jet said with a wave of her blinged-up hand, rings galore on every finger. They probably cost a fortune.

She was always done up to the nines with her acrylic nails and hair extensions, lovely makeup, designer clothes, and a fake-diamond-encrusted handbag where she always kept her gun or knife. No one would suspect her of being a leader or a gangster, which was probably why she'd opted to look the way she did. People who didn't know her wouldn't take her seriously. They had no idea she would slice your face quicker than you could blink.

"Of course," Pearl said, acutely aware that she had the air about her of someone who wouldn't be savvy enough to pay close attention to the person her boss was speaking to. In reality, she was adept at picking up on visual clues, expressions, inflections in voices, and all manner of things that would give her an insight into who Jet was dealing with, thanks to her mother and the profession she'd chosen, which she'd then foisted on Pearl who'd had to learn how to read people in order to survive some tricky situations.

When Andre had first started out, he'd gone by the name of Cola, probably a play on coke being the main thing he dealt in. This had been discovered by Jet's men doing their due diligence, but Andre must have decided that he wanted to go up a step in how he came across to people because he'd chosen to go with his real name recently. The use of Cola reminded Pearl of a man she'd become attached to in recent months, Mocha, who'd named himself such because he liked the drink.

She'd been abducted and taken to a house with boarded-up windows. Mocha and a man called Julian had kept an eye on her and the other women there. Pearl's only objective in becoming close to Mocha had been so she could hopefully steal the keys to the house and could escape. The women were locked in, so even if there had been a fire and the men weren't home, what with the shutters on the windows being screwed tight, everyone would have died.

When she'd eventually been freed by men in balaclavas coming to rescue everyone, she'd given her statement to the police and then gone home, wanting to forget about it all, but she'd stupidly missed Mocha until recently when she'd started working for Jet.

She pushed thoughts of him away. She was in yet another new phase of her life now, and looking back at the past did her no favours except to remind her of how stupid she'd once been in many respects. In each phase she always learned something new about herself, which she put to good use when she moved on into the next section. She quite liked where she was now and didn't particularly want to move on again, but her life had never been what you'd call stable, and she always had to roll with the punches and take whatever the world decided to dish out to her.

Jet flicked one side of her hair extensions over a shoulder. Some would probably say she looked plastic and unnatural, but underneath the put-together veneer was a shrewd businesswoman. Pearl admired her so much but was still shocked by how the fuck she'd ended up in her employ.

"Do you need me to get him talking on his own?" Pearl asked and briefly caught the eye of the driver in the rearview mirror.

He quickly looked away. Fucking perv.

"Let me see how the meeting goes first." Jet smoothed the trousers of her cerise suit. "If I think he's acting dodgy, then yes, I'll give you the signal to have a private chat."

Pearl had done it before. It wasn't as though she didn't have much experience with men, considering she used to be a sex worker, but then again, that would probably be considered a sex slave come the end. She knew how to get a man into bed but had no idea how to keep him there. Not once had she had a proper relationship—she didn't even include her nights with Mocha in that because despite them sharing secrets about themselves she'd been using him in order to nab those keys.

"Fine by me," Pearl said.

They continued the rest of the journey with Jet scrolling through cat reels on her phone and laughing while Pearl checked her recent messages that she hadn't had time to look at today. She opened the WhatsApp group called The Abductees.

It was a good job they all had a sense of humour really to be comfortable enough to call themselves that. Being abducted was a bloody serious thing and could have fucked them all up in a really bad way, but they were getting by. The other women, apart from Empress, had no idea what Pearl had been through in her life previous to being lured into the SUV. She hadn't opened up to them like she had with Alicia and Val. They belonged in another "section" of her life and had once been so dear to her, what seemed like many moons ago now. In some ways the other stuff she'd endured was worse than being snatched off the street and forced to perform in sex rituals.

At least those hadn't made her want to kill herself.

In her phone, Pearl had saved everyone as the names they'd chosen while working for the High Priest. Pearl had asked that they do the same for her. She didn't want to risk Candy and Fantasy knowing her real name and looking her up online, maybe discovering some of the shit that had happened to her. Empress knew a lot more about Pearl than any of them, what with being a police officer. Thankfully, she never bought up Pearl's darkest times in front of the others.

Some things, apparently, could remain a secret.

FANTASY: HOW IS EVERYONE?

EMPRESS: BUSY WORKING ON A NEW CASE.

CANDY: LOVING LIFE.

Pearl wasn't sure how to respond. They thought she was studying. They thought she'd given up sex work to pursue her dream of bagging a legit job where she could earn shedloads of money. She'd achieved that, it just wasn't legit. Not only did Jet pay her extremely well, but she gave Pearl the designer clothes, shoes, and bags she'd got bored with.

PEARL: STUCK IN TEXTBOOK HELL.

She was safe to make out she had her nose firmly wedged in a book. None of the others would go anywhere near the Proust Estate and catch her out in her lies, considering they all lived on Cardigan, and art exhibitions weren't exactly their thing anyway. Besides, she always looked so different when she was dolled up to go out with Jet who always insisted she paid for Pearl to get her hair done, plus the makeup, which, with all that contouring, meant she became a completely different person. As she hadn't seen them since their last catch-up in the café, they wouldn't know she now had blonde hair either, ditching the brunette.

After she'd been interviewed by the police, she hadn't intended to see the group ever again. Every time it was suggested that they meet up, she'd made excuses that she was too busy. In the end, she'd met them a few times at the French Café, but she felt she'd *really* moved on now. She should block their numbers and delete the chat really, but a little part of her liked the fact there was the illusion she had friends. They *were* friends, albeit ones who'd been thrown together, and they'd shared many conversations in the dark of their dormitory bedroom, but they weren't friends-friends. The others might think differently, considering they kept suggesting having drinks in the pub, going out for meals and whatnot, but every time Pearl saw them it just reminded her of yet another mistake she'd made. It was like poking a bruise when you knew it would hurt.

She didn't want to hurt anymore.

The driver eyed her up again in the mirror, and she glared at him until he was forced to concentrate on the road. If she told Jet how uneasy he made her, he'd be beaten up and sacked, but Pearl wasn't sure he deserved that just yet. Maybe he proper fancied her, not in a perverted way where he thought she'd open her legs for him, but honest to goodness taking a shine.

She wasn't sure how to feel about that.

She was seriously damaged goods.

He pulled into an alley between two buildings and parked round the back amongst the Audis, the Jaguars, and every other expensive car you could imagine. At first when Pearl had been exposed to this kind of lifestyle, she'd felt out of place and had the horrible urge to stand there crying whenever she got overwhelmed by the luxury. She didn't belong, that much was obvious, but Jet had taught her to pretend that she did.

"If you walk in anywhere acting like you own the place, head up, shoulders back, who the fuck would know you didn't?" Jet had said. "You show people what you want them to believe. You *tell* them what you want them to believe, got it?"

"So who *am* I?" Pearl had asked.

"Who do you want to be?"

"Someone who's important. I want to matter, and not just because I can make someone money. And that wasn't a dig at you by the way."

"I knew you meant your mother."

One of the stipulations of Pearl working for Jet was she had to tell her everything. Her story—or stories, because she viewed her life in sections—came out over a couple of hours having a meal at the Montreal, one of the many restaurants Jet owned and used as a front.

"Are you ready?" Jet asked.

Pearl nodded and opened her door, conscious of the driver's gaze on her as she walked round the back of the vehicle to meet Jet on the other side. *Did* he fancy her? Pearl threw her invisible cloak around her, the one stitched together with courage and bravery and 'I am worthy', telling herself she had every right to be there, the same as everyone else.

They walked around to the front of the building, the ground floor glass-fronted but with white panels hiding the view inside. Rumour had it a celebrity would be arriving at some point, which explained the heavy security presence standing around, men in black with radios clipped to their lapels and comms buds in their ears.

The usual greeter stood in front of the door, a man in a top hat and tails, which was another nod to something in Pearl's past. She forced herself to smile at him when his eyebrows shot up upon recognising her and Jet. He let them inside, and gone was the swoosh of a rain-drenched street with tyres turning over slick tarmac, replaced by the gentle murmur of voices belonging to elegant people who had so much money they didn't mind buying a painting that cost thousands of pounds. Even if Pearl had that kind of cash she wouldn't fork out on art costing that much. God, she'd felt posh when she'd bought a set of three canvases from Argos for seventy-five quid. Designer outfits were another matter, though, but she still wouldn't spend a grand on a pair of shoes like Jet did, but then she didn't have Jet's kind of income, did she. Two grand to Jet was like twenty pounds to Pearl.

The door closed, cocooning them in the sound of soft conversation, gentle laughter, and the scent of mixed perfumes and aftershaves. Jet made for the left to stand by the painting of a racehorse, the prearranged meeting spot. Pearl stood beside her, studying the brushstrokes on the horse's leg.

"Bloody hell, what's *he* doing here?" Jet muttered, moving so she also faced the painting.

"Don't turn around. I might have been lucky and he hasn't seen me yet."

Being told not to turn around made Pearl want to do it, but she knew better than to disobey her boss.

"Fancy seeing you here," a man said.

Pearl froze. She'd heard that voice before. Now was her chance to see who it belonged to, because last time they were in each other's orbit he'd had a balaclava on and waved a fuck-off scary machine gun in the air.

"Shit," Jet whispered and faced him.

Pearl did the same.

He stared at Pearl but did a semi-decent job of making out he didn't know her—but he did, even with her change of hair colour. She got the idea she ought to keep her mouth shut that they'd been formerly acquainted, his expression said as much, but surely she'd have to tell Jet that this man was one of those who'd dressed in army gear, carried a gun, and rescued her from that house.

"Good evening," Jet said. "What brings you here? It's a bit cultured for you, isn't it?"

"Cheeky fucking cow." He smiled at Pearl. "And who are you?"

"That's Pearl, my right-hand woman."

He made a choking sound.

"Something funny?" Jet barked.

"Not at all," he said. "Got a frog in my throat." He continued to smile at Pearl. "Right-hand woman, eh? Seeing as your boss isn't going to introduce me, I'm George, leader of Cardigan, and him over there is my brother."

What was she supposed to do now? Not telling Jet would get her into trouble if she ever found out Pearl had kept something from her, but going against The Brothers was another kettle of fish.

Fuck. Fucking fuck.

Chapter Three

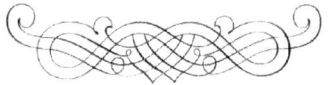

George had recognised Pearl the second he'd clapped eyes on her and had pondered on whether to walk back outside or go and have a chat. Having a chat was a bit dodgy, wasn't it? Considering they didn't want any of the people they'd rescued from the house to know it was them who'd been their knights in shining army fatigues, it was fucking stupid of him to go and introduce himself.

There was a problem with dithering and not making a decision as soon as you could. Jet Proust had spotted him, and he hadn't fancied her giving him a dressing-down at the next leader meeting for not going over to say hello. Now he had a quandary. Should he act like he didn't know Pearl or try to speak to her when Jet wasn't around? It was obvious she'd recognised his voice, the slight widening of her eyes had told him that. Fuck it, he was going to have to talk to her. He didn't want word getting out to the wider audience that they'd been involved, especially to that undercover copper.

"I'm here to meet a business associate," Jet said to him, "so if you could just fuck off, that would be great."

"Steady on. Fuck me, no need to be rude. I'd like a word with your right-hand woman before you leave."

"What for? She's mine, she's not available to be poached."

"I wouldn't dream of it."

"Then what's your business with her?"

Pearl appeared pensive, then she rested a hand on Jet's arm. "You know I told you about the men in balaclavas?"

Jet stared from Pearl to George. "Oh. Right. Then whatever you need to say to her, George, you can say in front of me. She's told me all about it. I should have realised it was you, but the army clothes and machine guns threw me off."

"That was the point." George looked at Pearl. "As you can appreciate, now that you work for Jet and understand how leaders deal with things, I'm sure you can manage to keep your mouth shut as to my involvement that night. We went in with disguises on for a reason."

Pearl nodded. "I've just got one question. How did you know where to find us?"

"It's a long story, one that doesn't need to be told."

"Where's Mocha?"

"That's two questions, and he's where he needs to be. I won't be drawn on the topic. You're safe now, Jet will look after you, and there's no need to harp on about our part in what happened."

"I feel the same way. This is a new start for me."

He frowned at her. "So why ask about Mocha?"

"I just wanted to know whether he was okay or not, that's all. He acted bad but he wasn't like that underneath it all."

Had she got attached to him? Was it a case of Stockholm syndrome?

George didn't fancy going through the ins and outs of Mocha's personality. As far as he was concerned, the saga was over, although he appreciated the situation would relive itself inside her head from time to time. Unless you were an expert in locking away your emotions, then shit like that didn't just fade in the memory.

"As I said, he's where he needs to be. Nice meeting you again." He walked away and found his brother admiring a painting of a rotten apple with a bite taken out of it.

"Did you bloody well see who I was just talking to?" George asked quietly.

"Yep. How did it go?" Greg asked.

"She recognised my voice, so now she knows we were there that night. I've made it clear our involvement isn't to be talked about."

"And if she does blab?"

That's easy. "I'd have to have a stronger word with her."

Greg eyed him. "Even though she's with Jet?"

"Yeah, and maybe Jet will need to be told to keep her lapdog in order."

"What's the deal with those two?"

"Pearl's her right-hand woman, would you believe."

"Fuck me, talk about a drastic change of fortune. I wonder how that came about."

That was something George was curious about, too. "God knows."

"Did you find out whether Pearl's still in contact with the undercover copper from the house? That could cause us problems now. Pearl might not outright say it was us, but she could drop hints."

"I assumed my gentle warning was enough, and considering Jet was standing there listening, it's not like I could get all nasty with Pearl, is it. We're on Jet's patch an' all, so I'd have to ask permission to be horrible to her, and of course, she'd say no."

Greg cocked his head at the painting. "I still think you should go back over and make it clear that the copper can't know it was us. One rotten apple can affect the whole basket."

"Hmm."

"I'll come with you."

As they approached the women, George put a hand out to stop Greg from going any farther. "Fucking hell, check out who she's doing business with."

Jet spoke to a man in his twenties, his black hair in a low ponytail, his suit a good cut. He'd certainly come up in the world from the little scrote they'd known a few years ago who hadn't had a pot to piss in. First Pearl had landed on her feet, and now this geezer. Was there something in the water?

"How the fuck did Scott move so high up in the world?" Greg muttered.

"Probably by doing the same thing as he used to do years ago except on a bigger scale."

"Drugs."

"At least he's stuck to his promise and stopped selling on our Estate."

"That we know of."

George grimaced. Greg had a habit of putting seeds into his head that had a propensity to grow into fucking great triffids, so now he wanted Scott followed from here and watched to make sure he wasn't dicking them about behind their backs. He might have said he wasn't selling on the Cardigan Estate, but there were plenty of back alleys and dark shadowy corners he could tout from. Some people would do whatever it took to get what they wanted, regardless of threats of violence and maiming and broken kneecaps. Whatever Scott had been up to, it seemed he'd done well for himself, but then George should know better than to judge a book by its cover.

"I wonder if he's as rich as he looks or whether the suit is just an illusion, something he's put on to give Jet the impression he's sophisticated rather than a twat."

"She doesn't suffer fools gladly; I bet this is their first face-to-face meeting and she's sizing him up just the same as we are. He's been sensible to get a good suit. First impressions an' all that. If we didn't know who he really was and he turned up to one of our meetings, he'd have my respect straight away before he'd even opened his mouth. They say clothes maketh the man."

"And they also say you can't make a silk purse out of a sow's ear."

Greg tsked. "That doesn't make sense. Scott looks like a silk purse is what I'm saying."

"Whatever he looks like, I don't want to do business with him."

"Only because we know who he really is under that suit."

George put himself in Jet's shoes. "Shall we tell her?"

"Yep, but she might not listen."

"Shall we tell her while she's still talking to him?"

"We can do."

George and Greg continued their way over, George catching Scott's eye. Scott appeared alarmed to see them, his expression going from assured to afraid, which meant Jet's attention swerved to where Scott was looking. She seemed to think his reaction was because he'd seen the twins in general—most people were scared of them so it made sense—but George was going to tell her different.

"*Not* nice to see you again, Scott," he said, stopping in front of him and looking him up and down. "I'd have thought coming to a place like this was way out of your league. You're more into paint by numbers, aren't you? You can buy shit like that in The Works, you know. What did you do, rent the suit and actually wash your hair? Did you get your mum to brush it and put it in that ponytail?"

Satisfied he'd insulted the bloke enough, George waited for the reaction. The Scott they knew would kick off, throwing his dummy out of the pram, but in this case it was probably best that he didn't respond and just walked away.

"I do not know what you are talking about," Scott said in an Italian accent.

It took George aback a bit. "Why are you talking like a ponce?"

Scott blushed. "I am here to do business with Miss Proust and I do not appreciate you butting in. It is rude and oafish."

Oafish! "If you were really some foreigner who didn't have a clue who I am," George said, "this would be about the time I ask you if you know who you're talking to. It would be a rhetorical question, one that would give you a clue that you're in the presence of someone you should show respect to, but as you're not a foreigner and you live on our Estate, and usually have a proper East End accent, and you know damn well who I am, I won't bother asking."

"What the *fuck's* going on?" Jet asked, her eyes narrowed. She placed a hand on her diamond-covered bag. She probably had a gun in there.

George felt a tad sorry for her so kept his voice down. There was no need for everyone else to hear what he had to say. "He's playing you. His name's Scott Talbert and he's most likely working on behalf of the real big boy at the top of the food chain."

Jet stared at Scott. "So you're not Andre Alexander?"

George laughed. "He most certainly is not. I think you need to go off and have a private little chat, don't you?"

"Don't tell me what to do, George," Jet snapped. "But yes, we do need a private chat, and if you don't mind coming along for the ride…"

Funny how she'd been rude and told him off, then in the next breath needed his help. Normally he'd take exception to that, but he was curious to see what was going to happen next. Their reason for being here in the first place had completely skipped his mind. He was going to have to shift their job onto someone else.

"Where are we meeting you?" he asked.

"The Montreal. Round the back—I don't want any of my customers seeing us taking him inside."

Scott darted his eyes around as though readying himself to run. The assured air he'd draped over himself as Andre Alexander seemed to have fucked off and left the country, much like Scott was better off doing after Jet had had a word with him. *If* she allowed him to leave the restaurant.

George glared at him. "Don't even think about it, sunshine."

"Please, modom," Scott appealed to Jet, still acting Italian for fuck knew what reason. Did he honestly think he could still pull this off? "I have no idea what this man is speaking of."

Jet kneed him in the bollocks. "Shut the fuck up, will you? Christ!"

Jesus, she doesn't muck about.

"Shall we take him in our car?" George asked her.

Jet nodded. "Please. I didn't bring any of my men with me tonight as I didn't expect trouble." She gave the doubled-over Scott a filthy look. "Our driver's waiting for us."

"How did you get mixed up with this twat?"

"I was assured he was on the level."

"Who by?"

"My men. They've been watching him. At his house, coming and going. I have photographs. I thought he was legit, and tonight was just about seeing whether I got on well with him in person like I did on the phone."

"He was seen at the house? Maybe he's got Andre's permission to pretend to be him. Or the person you saw at the house was the real one. It might be fun to find Andre and let him know."

Scott lunged forward, heading for the door. Greg stuck a foot out and tripped him over. Scott went flying and landed face-first, crying out in pain and rolling onto his back. Blood spewed from his nostrils, his nose skewed to one side. Art connoisseurs stepped back in alarm, whispering behind raised hands and looking at the three leaders as if they were scum. George ignored them and dragged Scott up to his feet, marching him outside and then round to the rear of the building. He held Scott's arms behind his back so Greg could cable tie his wrists, then they stuck him in the back of the BMW.

In the front, Greg said, "Why is it, wherever we go, trouble seems to find us? You're going to have to message our contact and tell her we won't be at the gallery when she arrives."

They were supposed to act as bodyguards after a rich Cardigan resident had purchased one of the paintings on the online auction. She didn't want to wait for it to be delivered and had insisted she'd take it home as soon as she'd bought it. George sent a message to their man, Moody, to get to the art exhibition and wait for the lady in question. He forwarded the photo she'd sent of herself to Moody so he'd recognise her, then he let her know there had been a change of plan and someone else would be looking after her. That reminded him to let Moody know about the code word she'd insisted on. This wasn't the kind of menial job they tended to do anyway. He should have suggested Moody from the start.

"You're going to regret this," Scott said from the back, still with a foreign accent.

George twisted round to look at him. "Pack it in, you dickhead, the game was up yonks ago."

Scott rested his head back and closed his eyes. "Fuck it."

"Fuck *up*, more like," Greg said. "Just think, if we hadn't been there tonight then you'd have got away with it. Did you think because Proust is a woman it'd be easier to pull the wool over her eyes? She'd have twigged something was up eventually, she's not thick, and she's just as bad as us when it comes to torturing the truth out people or beating the shit out of them for deceiving her. Now you've got the three of us on your case. Lucky you."

George smiled and watched the passing scenery. It didn't take long to get to the Montreal. George was hungry. He'd never been to any of Jet's restaurants, so tonight was as good a time as any to sample the food after they'd had a little conflab with Scott.

Maybe George would be able to work up more of an appetite if Jet wasn't in the mood to get her pink suit dirty, but on the other hand, he'd like to watch her in action.

Chapter Four

In the dark of a winter evening, where the air had a mind to freeze her face, Miranda dragged her feet on the way back from the corner shop. Reluctance to move forward pulled on her from behind like a tangible thing, as if it had hands to grip her arms with, holding her back. If that was really happening, she'd be fine with that, because going forward meant going home, and she didn't want to go there. She wasn't safe in that house, what with all the comings and goings, plus how men seemed to think they could treat her however they wanted. Mum had given them permission, making out they'd promised not to hurt her, but it was all a load of lies. How could a mum want her child to suffer through what amounted to rape? Just because Mum had given consent on her behalf, it didn't make it right.

Because of what went on inside it, Miranda had grown to hate that house with its outdated nineties wallpaper, sticky-back harlequin tiles on the hallway and kitchen floors, some of them peeling upwards on the corners, a trip hazard. Why the hell did the men even want *to visit a house as minging as that? It must be true what Mum said, that so long as sex was on offer, they'd ignore everything except the hole they were after.*

And the musty smell. No matter how much Miranda bleached the upper corners of every room where the damp crept in, that stench remained. What she wouldn't give to live by herself, but it wasn't likely that the council would offer her somewhere. She was single, didn't have any kids, and even though she'd tried to kill herself that time, she apparently wasn't classed as someone who had special enough needs to warrant that kind of help. Besides, what was it the letter had said? She was 'adequately housed' with her mother.

Adequately housed wasn't the way Miranda would have put it.

Maybe she shouldn't have lied when she was asked in the hospital what had made her take those tablets. Maybe she should have told the nice nurse what her mum had been forcing her to do. Maybe then she would *have special needs, and she definitely wouldn't be adequately housed. She could be given a flat, even a bedsit would do. She'd be free.*

She reckoned it was time to grow some balls and make her own way in life. She was old enough now, so Mum couldn't stop her from leaving. No more threats of the social coming to take her away. She could sign on for benefits, get one of those loans from the DWP so she'd have a bond to put down on a private-rented place. She couldn't stand to keep working for Mum, especially when she was paid fuck all. It wasn't fair, and she was so sick of her life that if she didn't claw her way out of it, she'd hopefully succeed in killing herself next time.

There was only so much she could take.
Strangers pawing her.
Breathing on her.
Licking her neck.

She took her time walking down one of the avenues with its nicer cars and front gardens compared to where she lived. Sometimes she played a game where she imagined she was someone else who had a proper job, mates to go out with on the weekend, maybe a bloke she actually wanted *to have sex with rather than feeling sick with the current ones Mum sent her way. Rapist bastards.*

Surely the women who lived behind these *doors weren't forced into sex, but then she shouldn't be so sure. There were those stories Miranda read in Mum's trashy magazines, people whose husbands didn't understand the word no. Sadly, one of them had taken their bloke to court, but it had been thrown out because she couldn't prove it was rape. No wonder she didn't trust men when shit like that was allowed to happen.*

At the end of the road, she turned left into her own street, cringing at the state of it. People had no respect along here. She supposed that if the roughness of it still bothered her then she couldn't be doing too badly up top. If her mental health was in a worse condition then she probably wouldn't even notice the mattress and fridge in the front garden over there or the smashed bathroom window in number ten.

If she cared, even if it was to be embarrassed, then there was hope for her yet, although saying that, caring meant you got hurt, you felt things, and she didn't want to. Best to be numb.

She took her keys out of her coat pocket and braced herself for entering the house. Christ, how many times had she stood here with the urge to turn and run? It was awful and overwhelming, made worse because where would she go? There was no one else in her life apart from her mother. She didn't include her absent father as someone to run to because he may as well not exist. Without a name, she couldn't find him. Mum had lied when she'd said if Miranda had sex with the men she'd tell her who her dad was. It had been nothing but a carrot dangling on a stick.

What about the police? Would they even help her or give a toss about what she'd been through? She doubted it. Mum had said no crime had been committed because Miranda had been of age when she'd first started working for her. She'd intimated plenty of times that if anyone ever asked, she'd tell all and sundry that Miranda had chosen *to have sex with those men. Miranda could refute that, but she didn't know if she even had the energy to fight.*

She looked around. As there were always so many cars parked down this street, she couldn't tell whether Mum's customer had come and gone yet. She prayed she didn't hear them going at it upstairs. God, could she have just one night where the sounds of sex didn't feature? It was her night off (apparently she was supposed to be grateful for it), and if she had any friends she would have gone to their house to remove herself from the toxicity for several hours, but she didn't, and it wasn't like she had the courage to walk into a boozer on her own, was it.

Maybe she should find that courage somewhere. She might actually get a life then. All of her daydreams could become a reality if she put her mind to it. But it was easier to comply, do what Mum said. There was a warped safety in continuing doing what you knew. Better the devil you know an' all that.

She stood in front of the door and cocked an ear, straining to pick up any noises. There weren't any coming from inside, but that didn't mean the bloke had gone. Some of them paid extra to lie there in bed afterwards, slagging off their boring wives or moaning about what had gone on at work. Tonight's man could be doing that.

She took a deep breath and let herself in, closing the door and again listening for sounds. The house stood in silence, too silent, the prickly kind that seemed to be able to breathe with a life of its own, so much so that it gave Miranda the creeps. The faint scent of aftershave lingered in the hallway from where the man had either come in just after she'd gone to the shop, or if he'd been a five-minute wonder, he'd recently left. All the lights were off, so unless Mum had gone out for the night with the customer to maximise earnings by playing at being an escort, then the place being in darkness wasn't normal.

Miranda didn't dare call out, because if Mum was in bed with yet another bloke she'd be pissed off at being disturbed. Instead, she took the carrier bag into the kitchen and put the shopping away, using the battery-operated light under one of the wall cupboards to see. She'd bought bread, milk, and cereal, plus orange juice.

Mum wouldn't bother paying for her half of it, she never did. Miranda had no idea why each of them played that particular game, Mum asking her to nip to the shop and saying she'd pay her later, when they both knew she wouldn't.

There had been so many instances where Mum had said something and Miranda had believed it would happen. Telling her who her father was; paying half for the shopping; giving her the whole weekend off. None of it had come true. Miranda fell for it every time and didn't understand why when she'd always been let down. Maybe it was hope that kept her believing that maybe one day, if only once, Mum would stick to her word.

Shutting the light off, she removed her shoes and coat at the bottom of the stairs, putting them away in the old walnut wardrobe, then carried her handbag up to her room. She popped it on her bed and sat there for a moment, frowning. Mum's bed didn't knock against the wall. No giggles came from the room next door. No deep rumbly voice of a customer told Mum what to do to him. And something didn't smell right. Miranda sniffed to try and determine what it was, racking her brain but coming up empty. A nasty feeling in her gut told her to go and check on Mum, so she got up and walked along the landing. She paused outside the bedroom door, fist raised ready to knock, and caught a whiff of that smell again.

Her stomach rolled over.

She reached out and switched the landing light on, staring in shock at a bloodied handprint on the doorframe, positioned as if someone had placed their palm and fingers on it with their back to the landing as they'd stared into Mum's bedroom. She registered the handle also had blood on it; she shouldn't touch it, she should do the right thing. But 'doing the right thing' meant she'd have to ignore what the police would prefer her to do. She pulled her sleeve down until her fingers were covered and turned the handle. Pushed the door open.

The landing light spilled inside the bedroom, Miranda's elongated shadow stretching across the bed and bending upwards on the wall—such a stupid thing for her to focus on when her heart hammered hard and the stink of blood lived in the air. Where was her mother? She stared at the splashes of scarlet on the rumpled cream bedding and the pillows with head dips in them. At the red bloodstains on the opposite wall where droplets had been thick and heavy and had dribbled down.

Sick to her stomach and with cold fear rushing through her, Miranda went into the bedroom, keeping her hands up beneath her chin so she didn't touch anything, sidestepping along the bottom of the bed. She needed to see the floor on the other side beneath the window. If Mum wasn't there, then she'd have to be somewhere else in the house. Or maybe, because she was obviously hurt, she'd run to a neighbour for help. But what if the punter was the hurt one? Shit, what if Mum had stabbed him with the ice pick she kept in her bedside drawer for the nights when someone got a bit too big for their boots and became violent towards her?

The blonde hair came into view first. Blonde hair with crimson streaks. Then the discarded hammer that had a blob of pinkish flesh on the claw end. Fuck. Fuck! The customer could have had long blond hair. It might not be her mum.

And Miranda might just be lying to herself.

A sob popped out. She moved along a bit more, Mum's ear, eye, and cheek becoming visible, spattered with blood. One more step, and Miranda stared at her whole face, ruined on the other side closest to the bed base. It had been caved in, the skin obliterated, the eyeball no longer there. Half of her nose skin was missing. It was as if an invisible line had been drawn down the middle of the face to leave one side perfect and the other wrecked.

A scream brewed, building and building in Miranda's chest until she thought she'd go mad if she didn't let it out. She clutched the sides of her head and released the noise, screaming until her throat hurt, her pulse throbbed too fast, and her legs threatened to give way. She shivered, a full-body tremble taking over.

Mum, on the floor. Dead. So fucking dead.

How was she supposed to feel? Was she meant to want to get down on her knees and try to bring her mother back to life? Was it normal for her own safety to be more important than anything else? Would other sons or daughters think of their mother first, themselves second? Probably, if they had good mothers who deserved having their child's breath forced into their lungs through CPR.

Miranda didn't want to go anywhere near her mum.

She stumbled out of the room and downstairs, only now aware that someone banged to be let in. The sound of her pulse thumping inside her head had drowned out anything else. She used her clean sleeve over her hand to open the front door, conscious that while she was trying to preserve evidence, she could have now wiped it away, her good intentions worth fuck all. Despite having a bitch of a mother, she still wanted the police to be able to catch who had done this. Was it too selfish of Miranda to be glad she'd been at the shop? One, so she didn't get killed herself, and two, she had an alibi. The neighbours were so nosy around here that someone would have seen her leaving and coming home, noting the times.

Oh God, everyone was going to come out and have a nose soon, weren't they? The police were going to turn up, and when that happened down here it was an excuse to stand with your cup of tea and watch the proceedings.

Miranda got her head back in the game and stared at the woman in front of her. Bunty, the forty-something from next door, stood on the path holding a silver torch. Mum had never got along with her, but Bunty had once said to Miranda if she needed any help she'd be there for her. Had she known, all this time, all those nights, what was going on in this house? It had to be obvious, didn't it, with the amount of men who came in and left half an hour later, that this was a knocking shop. Mum had told Miranda never to accept anything from the 'nosy bitch', not even so much as a teabag, but looking at Bunty now, Miranda could only see concern in her expression. She wasn't here to find out any gossip.

"What the hell's happened, love? I heard you screaming." Bunty looked ghostly with the torchlight pointing upwards beneath her chin. She'd probably done that so Miranda could recognise who she was, seeing as the bulb in the streetlight between their houses had been busted last week by kids throwing rocks.

Had Mum screamed? If she had, why hadn't Bunty heard it? Had she only heard Miranda's?

"My mum…"

Miranda had to get out — the smell of the blood, the customer's aftershave, the mould…it was too much. She'd be sick if she didn't get some fresh air. She flapped her hand for Bunty to move out of the way, and the woman stepped to the side. Miranda staggered down the garden path, snatching the gate open so she could go and stand on the pavement. Hands on her knees, she took a deep breath in, let a long breath out, then she remembered she'd left her phone in her handbag on her bed. The police would look at it. They'd see all the messages from the men where they'd booked appointments.

They'd know she was a prostitute.

No. She was going to have to say they were her friends. She couldn't stand the shame. And she couldn't stand the thought of them coming back when everything had died down, cursing her for letting on that they were paying her for sex. It caused trouble for them if their wives found out. Miranda just couldn't be doing with the hassle it would bring. She'd have to be like her mother and lie. But wouldn't they see the same numbers in Mum's phone and put two and two together?

"*The police,*" *she said,* "*we need to phone the police.*"

"*Wait there while I go inside and see first.*"

Miranda opened her mouth to tell her exactly *what she'd see and to not bother setting eyes on it for herself, but the words wouldn't come.*

Bunty went in then came out pretty quickly, her breathing laboured, muttering, "*Oh my fucking God!*"

over and over, taking her phone out of her bra and dialling nine-nine-nine.

Time seemed to skip with Miranda standing on that pavement with a crying Bunty beside her, no words spoken, or if there were, Miranda didn't register them over the sound of blood rushing inside her and the thud of her erratic pulse.

She sank into nothingness. Seeing nothing, feeling nothing. Floating.

The air ahead turning blue with intermittent flashes brought her back to what had happened—the comforting void she'd disappeared into no longer existed, and she now stood in the real world where a very real murder had happened.

Because there was no way Mum had survived that. No way she could still be breathing.

Everything seemed to zoom in around her all at once. Noise—chatter, the scuff of slippers on pavement, a bark of laughter that didn't belong; it was obscene considering someone had died so brutally. Someone? It was strange she didn't think of it as her mother who had been murdered, just some stranger, but maybe that was her mind's way of protecting her from the horror. If she distanced herself emotionally from the person she'd seen on that bedroom floor, then she might not have nightmares, she might not need to take a handful of pills and end it all.

A police car came to a stop beside the snake of cars outside the house, an ambulance a second or two behind it. Everything happened in a flurry then, officers and paramedics rushing into the house, neighbours shooting out of theirs to come over to Miranda and Bunty to ask what was going on, like they had a right to answers. Some stood at their open front doors, watching the drama. Miranda glanced along the row on her side of the street. Faces pressed to upper windows, breath creating condensation clouds. A neighbour or two in their gardens with their hands beneath their armpits to keep warm. One had even come out with a blanket draped over her shoulders and a cup of tea in hand, but then Miranda had known this would happen, she'd bloody predicted it, so why did it all seem so wrong?

More police arrived, and one of them, a man in a suit, asked Miranda and Bunty questions. Miranda felt as though she were underwater, all her faculties lost—the recall of what she'd seen came out in jagged sentences, the scene out of sequence. She vaguely picked up on the fact that Bunty was talking, then one of the uniformed officers came out of the house and spoke quietly to Mr Suit, probably telling him there was a body on the bedroom floor.

"Jesus Christ," Suit said. "Get this lot back into their gaffs, the nosy bastards, and I want a cordon set up. I also want a dog brought in to see if it can pick up a scent on which way the fucker went."

Someone steered Miranda into Bunty's—she had no idea who it was because she didn't look up from the ground, the underwater feeling still there, her pulse sloshing around along with her thoughts and the flashes of memory of what she'd been exposed to in the bedroom. She was going to have to tell Suit there was a customer. He'd be spoken to. Fucking hell, he could have been the killer, or Mum might have let another one in and it was them. The problem was, she couldn't remember who was supposed to be visiting tonight, so she'd have to tell Suit to look in Mum's notebook to get the information he needed.

And she was going to have to tell them what Mum did for a living. But that was the least of her worries. Her main concern was that if the killer wasn't caught he'd come back for her. And wasn't that another layer of selfish? She should be bothered about what Mum had been through, what her last moments had been like, but she found she didn't care.

Life would be better without her mother in it.

Chapter Five

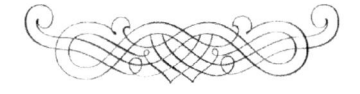

Pearl hoped she'd made the right decision by outing George in front of Jet. It'd certainly been the right decision from Jet's point of view but not necessarily George's who could possibly have wanted his participation in rescuing everyone in that house kept a secret from a fellow leader. The thing was, Pearl had decided she liked her life as it was, thank you very much, and any threat George might make wouldn't mean anything because she was under Jet's protection. Better to not bite off the hand that fed you.

In the car on the way to the Montreal, Jet pressed the button to raise the glass between the front and back seats. It reminded Pearl of when Mocha's SUV had been modified after Tara had escaped from the moving vehicle.

"Before we left, I forgot to thank George and Greg for rescuing you," Jet said. "If they hadn't, then me and you might not have met. You know you're not going to be able to tell anybody what they were up to that night, don't you. What leaders sometimes do is something best kept away from the general public."

Her voice held a warning tone, one Pearl heeded.

"I gathered that. They did me a huge favour, so I'm not about to tell anyone what they did. I can understand why they wouldn't want anyone knowing they've been involved, especially since some of the main players have been removed from the equation."

"You said Julian had gone into hiding with his wife and sons, their names changed, and that

Mocha had disappeared. You probably realise now what's really happened to him."

"They likely killed him, didn't they?"

Jet nodded. "I'd have done the same because he murdered those innocent women. He might not have wanted to, but he did, and regardless of his situation and the fact that he didn't have any choice, he still needed to pay for taking those lives."

"Do you think the same should have happened to Julian?"

"No, because although he watched and helped dig the graves, he didn't actually pull the trigger."

Pearl wasn't going to revisit the comment about Mocha not having any choice. It was unfair that Jet thought he had to pay for something he had no control over. How could he have refused to shoot those women when the High Priest stood there breathing down his neck? Not to mention the fact that the High Priest had threatened to kill Mocha's mother if he didn't do whatever he was told. If Pearl argued the toss with Jet, then they'd end up falling out, and that was never fun because Jet was brilliant at giving the silent treatment.

No one would ever understand why Pearl agreed that Mocha should have been allowed to walk free. According to Empress, his mother had also gone missing; her team had surmised that the pair of them had run away together. Pearl had asked George where Mocha was so she could get an inkling of the truth. Him saying that Mocha was where he needed to be…could she take it that he was alive and living away from London? Maybe, like she'd tried to do regarding her mother's death, she should lock it all away in a box and pretend it never happened.

"Mocha was between a rock and a hard place, but I'd still have bumped him off," Jet continued. "Some loose ends fray a bit too much if they're left to their own devices. George would have made the decision based on the information he had at the time. I expect Mocha would have been interrogated. He might have admitted to doing other things that the twins couldn't turn a blind eye to. They probably felt it was best all round to just get rid."

That was fair enough, and Pearl knew she would always find that decision unfair because of the time she'd spent alone with Mocha, how she knew him better than any of the others had. No matter that he'd shouted at her sometimes, especially at the beginning when she'd just been settling into her new life in the house, he still didn't deserve to die.

What Pearl really wanted was help in discovering whether Mocha's disappearance was just an illusion. It wasn't that she wanted him to come back and be in her life, it was because she wanted the cold hard facts that he could *never* be in her life. Not now she'd got this job, had money to play with; she didn't want anybody to swan in and fuck it up. He might do that if he reappeared. But then was she being big-headed here? Who was to say he'd even want anything to do with her? He'd likely been using her as much as she'd been using him. She'd wanted a key in order to escape, he'd wanted sex and someone to talk to.

"That copper I told you about," Pearl said, "the one who was undercover, she said Mocha's mum has also gone."

"Then it sounds like they were banished as a pair. Told to fuck off and not come back. Live under assumed names."

Pearl felt better now. Banished meant they couldn't come back, and if they did and they were caught, they'd be killed. Or maybe the twins didn't want to kill them at all and they felt that banishing them was the only way it would stop Mocha from being recognised and arrested. But he could be arrested anywhere. Or had he grown his hair and now had a long beard?

Stop giving a shit. Close the door and lock it.

She stared out of the window as the car entered the food strip, one long road full of restaurants and takeaways. Interior lights shining through the plate-glass windows of kebab and pizza shops lit up the tatty pavements, while the creamy tones from expensive restaurants gave off a more muted glow. People hung around eating food out of containers with wooden forks, soaking up the night's alcohol, and Uber Eats delivery people darted from their bikes to the shops and back again, zooming away in a burst of whining engine noise.

This slice of life was what Pearl had missed while she'd been in the house, the ability to just walk out and go somewhere to buy food. Fantasy's main beef had been not receiving Amazon parcels—and not being paid any money in order to afford to *buy* Amazon parcels. Candy had claimed to love living there, although these days, now she had a new flat and had become really good friends with Fantasy, her life was a hell of a lot better and she could admit now that she must have been insane to want to stay in the boarded-up house forever.

It had been such a surreal time.

The Montreal stood two buildings from the end, a majestic castle with its fake turrets on the frontage that was done up to resemble old stone. Two men stood either side of the studded wooden door in black suits and ties, white gloves and shirts, their hair slicked back with comb lines in it. They were there to either intimidate or reassure, to keep people away or let them in, depending on whether they had a reservation or not. If your name's not down you're not coming in.

Jet's driver stopped outside. He never got out to open the doors for them as Jet felt the gesture was archaic, although she did understand the sentiment. Pearl left the vehicle, Jet getting out and jerking a thumb at a door that had been disguised as part of the building and blended seamlessly with the stones. One of the security men used the keypad on his phone on an app. The stone door swung inwards, and on the other side, Eddie waited for them beneath the fairy lights strung up on the alley wall of the restaurant next door. Jet closed the door, and they followed Eddie down to a courtyard which had tables used in the summer, the parasols stored in a nearby shed disguised to look like a small castle. Double iron gates in the surrounding turreted wall stood open and led to a lit car park.

Eddie was in charge of this whole area.

"I have three guests who need escorting to the cellar," Jet said to him. "Two are welcome, one is not, if you get my meaning. You'll understand exactly who is who once you see them. We'll go down and wait."

Jet walked into the building, waiting for Pearl in the corridor with several doors. Two were for the public toilets, one for the stairs to her office and the flat above, another to the bar and restaurant areas, and lastly, one for the cellar.

She unlocked it and flicked the light on, making her way down the stairs. At the bottom, she waited for Pearl to join her and passed her a gun from her sparkly handbag. As was normal in these situations, because the door had been unlocked and left open, there was a chance a customer might accidentally come down, despite there being a plaque on the door that said

PRIVATE. Drunk people didn't always read signs, and Pearl was there to make sure they did.

She stood facing the stairs with the gun aimed towards the top. She hadn't had to shoot anyone yet, but there was a first time for everything, and she was confident she'd remember what to do since Jet had taught her how to use the weapon. Never in her wildest dreams had Pearl thought she would a) be trusted enough to be given a gun, and b) have the guts to use it, but if a threat appeared at the top of the stairs and Jet told her to shoot, then she'd fucking well shoot.

Jet unlocked the door to the torture suite beside Pearl. The door next to it led to the beer cellar, the faint sounds of the mechanisms clicking filtering through. Pearl could just imagine Andre's shock when he saw where he'd end up, but then according to George he wasn't called Andre, was he. Jet was going to go mental once she confirmed she'd been lied to—or would she play it the other way and be deadly calm? Pearl could never work out which version frightened her more.

Before they'd set out tonight, and while she was getting ready, she'd had an uneasy feeling inside her. It seemed her instincts had been right.

Something bad *was* going to happen tonight, but not to her or Jet as she'd originally imagined. She'd thought going to the art gallery was a bad idea but hadn't voiced it to her boss because, let's face it, Jet would have gone anyway as Pearl didn't have any facts to base her unease on.

While she waited for someone to appear at the top of the stairs, she recalled the first time she'd seen the torture suite. Jet had given her a tour of all the places they'd frequent the most while Pearl was at work, and the room to her right was the weirdest of them all as it didn't look like a torture suite. In the centre, a metal morgue table, with straps for the wrists and ankles. A set of four drawers in the wall to hold dead bodies to be taken away and disposed of later. A hidden door disguised as part of a panelled wall—Jet liked her fake doorways—led to a room built beneath the back yard. The only furniture in there was a Formica-topped table and a stack of blue plastic chairs, the accused sitting on one side, Jet and whoever she asked to join her to help interrogate on the other.

It could all be very civilised if no voices were raised and certain devices weren't used. Those were stored on the wall behind the interrogator, weapon after weapon hanging on hook after hook, placed there so the person being spoken to had a bloody good idea of what was coming their way if they didn't respond in the manner Jet wanted them to.

The door at the top of the stairs opened a couple of inches, putting Pearl on high alert. She secured her finger around the trigger, ready to fire if need be, but as the gap widened and George appeared in the frame, she lowered the gun and stepped back into the corner of the little rectangular floorspace to allow them to go into the torture suite first.

George came down the stairs with Andre/Scott behind him, Greg following. Still standing at the top was Eddie. He waited for the nod from Pearl after the three men had entered the suite, then he shut the door. She waited for the sound of the lock engaging before she proceeded into the suite and leaned against the closed door, the gun loose by her side, but she'd raise it if she was given the go-ahead. Jet had opened the secret door and gestured for the guests to go through. George put his head in, probably to check it was okay first, then he looked over his shoulder and gave his brother a nod. Greg went inside after George, tugging the bloody-nosed drug dealer with him.

"Sit him on the chair that's already out," Jet said, "and if you want to take a perch yourself then get one from the stack."

She wandered into the room, waving her hand up beside her head to let Pearl know she wanted her to join the meeting. Pearl went in and again leaned on the closed door. The drug dealer sat at the table, Greg's hands on his shoulders keeping him seated. George collected four chairs, placing three of them on the opposite side of the table and then carrying one to Pearl.

"I take it she's allowed to sit," he asked Jet who nodded.

Pearl thanked him and took a load off.

Jet collected two pairs of handcuffs from the wall and clipped the end of each to the victim's wrists, then the other ends were attached around the front chair legs so he was in a hunched-over position, likely uncomfortable. If he was quick enough, he could manage to free himself by standing and tipping the chair back, but that's where the gun would come in handy. Pearl would probably be instructed to shoot him in the foot.

Greg sat to the right of the middle seat and George to the left. Jet returned to the wall and picked a small taser, one that didn't have wires. It resembled a man's shaver and had a conductor that gave a jolt of pain when pressed against the skin. She fired it up so it crackled and gave the bloke the idea of what was to come, moving to stand behind him, holding the weapon by his neck.

"If you want to play Fuck About and Find Out, when I ask you a question you're going to give me a false answer, but if you don't want to play that game, you'll tell me the truth."

"What's Fuck About and Find Out?" George asked.

Jet smiled. "It's where people dick me around, and then I have to hurt them until they stop dicking me around. Some people like to play it for so long that by the time I've got to their bollocks and zapped them, they wish they were dead because they *hurt* all over. You'd think they'd just tell the truth from the start, wouldn't you, because then they wouldn't be in so much pain, but there's some strange folk about, and what they choose to do is their business. It's not me screaming in agony, is it, so what do I care? Tell a lie…"

She leaned down so the victim knew she was talking directly to him now. "I *do* care if I've got somewhere to be. I care when I make plans and they get ruined or delayed. Like tonight for instance. After we'd had our little meeting at the art gallery, me and Pearl were going to be having a meal upstairs. We'd probably be there by now, prawn cocktail as a starter for me, ciabatta with sun-dried tomatoes for her, a nice cold glass of white wine each."

She rested the weapon on his neck but didn't push the button.

"But instead of doing that," she said through gritted teeth, "I'm down here with some fucking ponce of a liar who decided to steal someone's name, his identity, and his accent to try and fool me into buying drugs from him instead of the real deal. I would have done it, too. I believed everything you said to me prior to setting eyes on you tonight. You even *look* like the real Andre Alexander. And it's made me feel very stupid. I don't like feeling stupid."

He sniffled.

"Now, you might wonder why I haven't done due diligence and contacted a few people in the know on the journey here to confirm who you really are, but here's something you might not be aware of. Leaders may well run different parts of London, and from time to time they may well not get on. There've been feuds and murders amongst them, but despite all that, when it comes down to the wire, unless you're dealing with an absolutely treacherous cunt, when they tell you the person you're meeting isn't who he claims to be, you believe them, so there's no need to double-check."

George seemed pleased about that statement, giving her a nod. "We caught this bloke selling drugs on our Estate without permission years ago. We told him the rules and what needed to be done, but unfortunately, he wasn't prepared to pay protection money. We let him know he could no longer work on our patch and if he was caught doing so we'd kill him. In the meantime, I beat him up, broke both his arms, and sent him on his way. We haven't seen hide nor hair of him until tonight."

"So," Jet said, "are you Scott or Andre?"

"I swear to God I am Andre."

"Oh dear," she said and pressed the button.

Chapter Six

George like Jet's style. Of course he did, she reminded him of himself. For once, he didn't itch to take over. He'd happily sit there and watch her deal with Scott, and afterwards he'd suggest, if it didn't piss her off too much, that they join her upstairs for dinner. The mention of prawn cocktail had his mouth watering.

Scott screeched from the pain he experienced from the little taser, and Jet removed it from his skin.

"I'm going to ask you again," she said, "Are you Andre or Scott?"

"Andre!"

"Where were you born?"

"Naples."

"When did you move to England?"

"Years ago."

Jet shook her head. "What have you done, memorised the bloke's life and stepped into his expensive shoes as though you've got every right to wear them? How did that even happen? Going by what I've heard about Andre, you'd have been met with resistance if you rocked up at his gaff ready to take over everything he owns and who he is. Or is that *was*? Did you have to kill him?"

"I am Andre."

George snorted. "You do look like him, I'll give you that much, but I recognised you straight away. You must be dealing with people who've never met him before in order to get away with it."

"Like me." Jet pressed the button and let him have another burst of pain.

Scott screeched again and drummed his feet on the floor. George didn't get what the geezer was playing at. It was obvious he'd been caught for what he done, and yet he was still trying to convince them he had Italian blood running through his veins.

"I'm not trying to teach you how to suck eggs, and don't go having a mare at me, but what due diligence *did* you do?" George asked Jet.

Thankfully, she didn't look like she was about to explode at him for being rude. "The usual surveillance for a few weeks. Had my best men on it. They took photos."

"Do you still have them?"

She nodded and took her phone out of her bag. Swiped until she found them, then showed George the screen.

In every image, Scott had sunglasses on.

"I can see how he got away with it," George said. "With the specs, and the angles these photos were taken from, yeah, he's a dead ringer. We'll pay the real Andre a visit later, that'll solve things."

"What if he's not there, though?" Pearl said. "The surveillance that was done was outside Andre's house. 'Andre' appeared every so often for a photo opportunity, got in his car but returned quickly, then went back inside. Are you assuming Andre has employed Scott to pretend to be him? Because if Scott took over by force, then I doubt very much Andre's going to be there, is he."

"Fair point," George said. "We'll still go to the house regardless. Andre could be tied up and all sorts."

Jet put her phone away and poked a finger in the air towards Scott. "This one will be dead long before then because I'm not in the mood to fuck about this evening. If you say he's Scott then he's Scott. I just want him to admit that."

She walked over to the wall. George craned his neck to watch her put the taser on its hook and select cutters suitable for snipping off the ends of fingers, except when she returned to Scott she didn't crouch to take one of his hands in hers. Instead, she gripped his hair in a fist and cut off his top lip which dropped between his open legs and landed on the floor. Scott's scream was the type that really sliced into the old eardrums, and it got on George's wick.

"Shut your fucking mouth," he barked at him. "There's no need to be so loud."

Jet laughed and lopped off Scott's bottom lip. Blood pissed everywhere, down his chin and onto his trousers. Jet let his hair go. He got up and managed to throw the chair off the cuffs, rushing towards Pearl who raised the gun.

"Don't come any closer or I'll shoot you in the dick," she shouted above the din he was making.

Scott appeared to believe her as he stopped short and dithered, then darted towards the tools and weapons on the wall, the handcuffs swinging. Pearl glanced to Jet for instruction. Jet nodded, and Pearl aimed the gun and fired. The noise of the retort stunned Scott silent until the agony kicked in where she'd shot him in the foot. He collapsed onto his knees, wailing, Jet going up behind him and grabbing his ponytail. With surprising strength for a woman her size, she dragged him back to his chair and forced him to sit on it, then she got right in his face.

"You just made a big fucking mistake, you little prick."

His lipless, bloodied mouth moved as though he tried to speak, but all that came out were whimpers through clenched, scarlet-stained teeth.

"What's that?" she asked. "Are you trying to tell me that your foot hurts, and your gob hurts, and probably your *feelings* are hurt? I couldn't give a fuck, mate. You tried to trick me. All right, if George hadn't recognised you, you may well have supplied the drugs and I could have paid for them and I wouldn't have been any the wiser that I was dealing with a scammer, but once I knew you weren't the real Andre, then things changed."

She went to the wall and selected a cheese wire, and George knew then that she was going to garotte the fucker, but there was no way she was going to be able to do it without getting blood on that suit. But she surprised him and, as though reading his mind, she placed the cheese cutter back on the wall and left the room, coming back wearing white plastic overalls, including a hood and gloves.

She picked up the cheese gadget again and stood behind Scott, draping the wire over his head so it rested above his Adam's apple. She gripped the wooden handles tight and quickly whipped them downwards. The wire cut into his skin and flesh, blood oozing down in a sheet. Scott choked on it, scarlet speckles floating in the air on a cough, George and Greg scooting their chairs back to get out of the way of the spray. Jet turned her face to one side, maybe so it didn't get spattered, and gave a massive yank so the wire ate into his throat. As George had thought earlier, she had such strength for a small woman. On the second forceful tug, she'd almost perfected a decapitation.

She let the handles go and moved over to the rear corner. Pearl pressed a button beside the weapons, and the ceiling above Jet opened in a small square and a showerhead came out. Pearl pressed another button, and water cascaded down. Jet doused her plastic outfit to get all the blood off, avoiding getting her face wet—she probably didn't want to ruin that nice makeup job she had going on. The pink water headed into the corner where, now George studied it properly, the floor dipped slightly. It disappeared into a gully, then into the grate of a drain.

George and Greg moved over to the door. The water stopped, and Jet took her plastic outfit off, discarding it on the floor. She walked over to them, clean as a whistle, and flapped a bejewelled hand at Scott.

"I'll get someone to take over Eddie's shift outside so he can come and deal with him. He'll pop him in the fridge and give this place a good tidy up. Thanks for bringing that little bastard here for me, I owe you one."

"Dinner will do," George said.

Jet sighed as though on the verge of losing her shit—going by her rant regarding her evening being disturbed by things going wrong, she likely didn't want to have them sitting at her dinner table. "I suppose I can stretch to that."

"Stretch? You're not skint, are you?"

She laughed. "I meant mentally stretch. There's only so much bandwidth I've got to deal with things, and that dead bastard almost depleted it all. But it's fine, I'm sure I'll manage for a couple of hours."

Chapter Seven

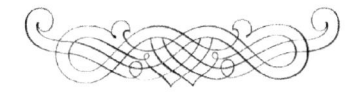

Miranda had never been to a funeral before. She imagined most dead people had a fair few mourners, genuine ones who'd actually cared about them when they'd been alive, but all Mum had was Miranda, Bunty, and two neighbours from over the road. Hardly an amazing turnout, but it was better than Miranda standing there all by herself with the

vicar, feeling like a spare part. Feeling exposed, the only one in the church the man of the cloth could look at. An ant beneath a microscope.

Fucking hell, it had been a tough, frustrating road since the murder. Firstly, finding out the killer was Mr Swanson, who'd been visiting the house for years and years, had been such a shock. She'd swear he didn't have it in him. And Miranda had been right in what she'd suspected when she'd smelled that aftershave — the original customer had come and gone. Mr Swanson had arrived afterwards on the off chance Mum could slot him in.

What she hadn't *suspected was Mum had told him to go home, stick to their agreement of seeing her once a week, but he'd talked her round. They'd had sex, and he'd brought up how he wanted her all to himself. She'd said no, and he'd lost the plot. He'd admitted everything, or enough that it matched the evidence at the 'crime scene' — weird and unsettling to think of Mum's bedroom like that — and he'd been carted off to prison. No trial, thank God, he wasn't disputing what he'd done.*

She hadn't even known whether Mum wanted to be buried or cremated, they'd never had that discussion, and there was no paperwork to give any indication, so Miranda had gone with whatever the lady at the Co-op

Funeral Services had suggested—a burial. It was more expensive than a cremation, but that didn't affect Miranda anyway. Bunty had helped her get the funeral costs paid for by the social.

Miranda had continued to see to the customers, her workload doubled with Mum not being there. It was nice to have so much money, considering she'd only ever been given a few quid here and there from her mother. She already had a stash of five hundred quid on top of the benefits Bunty had helped her claim. The rent was being paid by the council, and she'd arranged for someone to come in and clean the mess in her mother's bedroom, removing all the furniture, repainting the walls, and her next job was to buy a new bed, wardrobe, and carpet.

At the moment the room was empty, no trace of Mum left behind. Bunty had suggested that Miranda concentrated on that room in between the death and the funeral, which, she'd said, was the hardest stretch of time most humans had to endure. Limbo, she reckoned, when you came to terms with the death and then it fully hit you on the day you put your loved one to rest that they were gone, not coming back.

On the day Bunty had come round to help bag up Mum's clothes, Miranda hadn't even tried to explain her difficult relationship with her mother, how she loved her and hated her in equal measure. Actually, that wasn't true, she hated her more than she loved her. Bunty hadn't pried, so she wasn't 'nosy' like Mum had said, and they'd ended up chatting about mundane shit to pass the time.

It might be winter, but when they'd left the house this morning the sun shone, the sky a vibrant blue, a few puffy white clouds scudding along. One of them had looked like a dragon, and if Miranda were the fanciful sort, she'd say it was Mum letting her know there was something on 'the other side'.

She'd loved dragons.

It seemed a waste to open the church up for so few people, especially someone who'd forced her daughter into the sex trade. Miranda would never get over what she'd been subjected to and how she'd so naturally chosen to continue that profession even though Mum wasn't there to make sure she did. It was all she knew anyway, and now she was aware of how much money she could make from it, she doubted she'd ever do anything else.

She hugged herself, the church cold. The men from the funeral home had already carried the coffin up the aisle and placed it in front of the altar, sombre in their black suits, white shirts, and black ties. One of them had led the way tapping a walking stick on the flagstones with each step, his tall top hat giving him an imposing height, the tails of his suit jacket so long they reached the backs of his knees. The lady at the Co-op had talked Miranda through what would happen today, had even gone so far as to explain why there was such ceremony, but honestly, it all seemed a bit too posh and respectful for Mum.

A cruel thing to think but true.

As the vicar prepared to speak, he stared down the aisle and nodded at the sound of the door opening. Footsteps echoed, and someone sat in the pew directly behind Miranda. She wanted to turn around and see who it was, but the vicar launched into his speech, talking about Mum as though she were a pillar of the community and had never put a foot wrong. There was no mention of the sordid life she'd lived, just that she had a daughter who she'd brought up single-handedly. Hallelujah, what a saint.

They stood for a hymn, one Miranda didn't know the words to, and she didn't even pretend she did, keeping her mouth closed. She thought lots of other people must have come in because there were more voices singing than those present, but then she realised they were coming out of speakers hidden beside tall bunches of fake flowers inside Grecian urns.

Eventually, after what seemed like two hours but was probably only twenty minutes, the men in suits were back, and Mr Tappy Cane led them towards the doors while they carried the coffin outside. Miranda had turned to watch the procession leave and now glanced at whoever had come to stand behind her. It was one of Mum's customers who gave her a small nod. It looked like he'd been crying. Bloody hell, had he actually cared for her, got attached over the years like Mr Swanson?

What the hell had they seen in her?

It was time for Miranda to follow the coffin, Bunty looping their arms together. Once they were outside, they walked behind the slow-moving hearse with the coffin back inside it, presumably to the plot that had been reserved for Mum.

The next bit went by in a blur, then they were in Bunty's car—she'd suggested they go to and from the church in it so it would save on the funeral costs. Miranda had agreed because she didn't fancy getting in one of those big cars that ferried the family behind the hearse. With Mum now in the hole in the ground, Bunty drove them to the Blue Dolphin where they sat in a corner with sausage and chips plus gins in balloon glasses. The other neighbours hadn't joined them, nor had the punter.

"I'm sorry if my mum ever made you feel bad," Miranda said after at least ten minutes of silence between them.

"You shouldn't apologise for someone else's behaviour. Your mother chose to act the way she did, and it was no reflection on you. I have to say you need to be careful. A few of the neighbours twigged what your mum got up to, and there's been talk that you've been doing the same since she died. Not only should you be careful of letting strange men into your house, but there's the very real worry that someone's going to grass you up for running a knocking shop while you're also drawing benefits. I suggest you ask your customers to go round the back so no one in the street sees them."

"Thanks for letting me know. Not many people would."

"I'm old enough and ugly enough to understand that life doesn't always work out the way you thought it would and you have to do things you hadn't expected in order to survive. I doubt very much your mum imagined when she was a teenager that she'd end up on the game. She likely thought she'd be a hairdresser or whatever else used to be on offer to us at school when we filled out the college forms, but she found herself pregnant, and she made money in the easiest way she

knew how. I just wish she'd let me in, emotionally I mean, as a shoulder to cry on, as support, but she always called me a nosy cow, thought I only ever wanted to know her because I'd get some gossip, but that's not the case at all."

"I hate her for what she put me through, you know."

"I'm sure you do, but maybe, given time, the hate will fade and you'll either feel nothing or you'll be forgiving. We all have to make tough decisions, and I bet when your mum found out she was up the duff she had to make a few of her own. Stand in her shoes for a minute."

"I don't want to." That would mean Miranda would have to care. "She could have got help, could have brought me up in a better environment. Isn't that what should be the first thing on a mother's mind, her child and its welfare? Do you know, my first ever memory in that house is of her letting a man in. Mr Swanson, funny enough. He had a bunch of flowers for her, and she was so rude she laughed in his face, saying she was only letting him in for a shag, nothing else was on offer. I didn't know what that meant at the time, the shag thing. Maybe he wanted to be more than a customer even back then. If she'd accepted that, he

might have looked after both of us and I wouldn't be where I am now."

But was that true? He'd been prepared to have sex with Miranda when she was still classed as a child. Had he chosen Mum because she had a little girl? Had he wanted to groom her?

"Ever since I was sixteen," she continued, *"I haven't known anything else regarding work, and the weird thing is, I'm used to it now, it's become just something I do. There are no emotions involved anymore—well, there are, but the kind that come with working out how much you could earn on any given night and what debts you can clear with it."*

"I did wonder whether she'd left you in a bit of a financial hole."

"It's fine, I've already made enough to pay off the red bill reminders that came through the post."

"It's shocking, that's what it is, although I still can't help but feel sorry for her, but I mainly feel sorry for you. Things can still be different. You could still turn it around because you're so young. Do a course or two. Get qualifications."

Miranda didn't want to think about that, it required too much effort, and her brain was already overloaded from today. She felt bad that Bunty might be going through the same thing, tired out from the *funeral. "You don't have to sit here with me, by the way. I'll be fine if you need to get home."*

"If you're sure."

Bunty gave her hug, something Miranda didn't get many of, then she left the pub. Glad to be by herself, Miranda finished her gin and ordered another and another, and then somehow found herself in a conversation with a man who sat in Bunty's seat, saying he knew Mum pretty well and had been shocked that she'd been killed.

Was this how it was going to be? Whenever Miranda walked into a pub, would she get men reminding her that her mother had been a slapper? Would they do what this fella was now and ask her if she was on the game, too? Miranda didn't respond to him, she just didn't have the energy, and instead continued to drink.

Her mind became fuzzy. She accepted his offer of some white powder and went off to the toilet to sniff it. She'd never done it before, and the rush it gave her meant she kind of floated out of the loos and back to her seat. He said he had some marijuana that they could puff on in the corner of the yard at the back where all the smokers went. Fuck it, what did she have to lose? She followed him out there and had a joint, or maybe she had two, and then a couple more gins when they went back inside.

Then the maudlin phase hit. She put herself in Mum's shoes like Bunty had suggested. And that's when everything went a bit wrong.

Chapter Eight

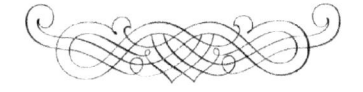

At dinner last night, which was bloody gorgeous (George had a steak), they'd agreed to visit Andre's home this morning, as Jet's 'bandwidth' had gone completely on the fritz not long after dessert had been finished and she had no energy left to snoop around at that time of night. George and Greg currently waited in their van outside the Italian's gaff, wigs, beards, and glasses on, plus trainers, tracksuit bottoms, and fleece hoodies. Andre lived on the Cardigan Estate, so to minimise any gossip, they were all dressing up to disguise their identities.

"Jet doesn't seem to be as fuming as I'd be," George said. "I mean, did you see how calmly she killed Scott? Either she's one of those psychopaths or she's got immense control over her emotions."

"Maybe that bandwidth she spoke about goes deeper. She could actually be an introvert playing at being an extrovert so she's used to pretending to be someone else while she's at work. Or it could be as simple as not being able to cope with too much fun at once."

"Yeah, and with her being a leader she has to hide the fact she's not always at the top of her game. Must be bloody exhausting. It wouldn't be a good idea to let anyone outside her circle of trust know that she's got vulnerabilities."

"Which means she trusted us, and Pearl, to have said what she did in front of us. About the bandwidth, I mean."

"Good to know. How about Pearl, though? She shot Scott without a hint of remorse. What the fuck's happened to her since we got her out of that house? How do you go from being a sex worker to a leader's right-hand woman?"

"No idea, but you're nosy enough to ask them."

George smiled, then that smile slipped when something dawned on him. "Martin's been coming here to collect protection money every week, so either someone else has been handing it over or he fell for Scott's disguise as Andre. I'm going to give him a ring and see what's been going on."

He took the phone out and prodded the screen to connect the call and then pressed the icon for it to go on loudspeaker.

"Martin? Andre Alexander. Fifteen Gelston Way. He gives you protection money every week, yes?"

"It's paid, but it isn't him who gives it to me, his girlfriend does."

George raised his eyebrows at Greg. "Does she now. What does she look like?"

"Young, black, those laminated eyebrows."

"Did you get a name off her?"

"Shawnee Devonshire—double E in Shawnee, not a Y, she was quick to point out."

"How long has she been handing the cash over?"

"A fair few months."

"Cheers."

George ended the call and slapped the dashboard. "So if this is what I think it is and we've got Scott impersonating Andre, then someone else being in on this makes sense because Scott wasn't exactly the sharpest tool, was he, and if something's happened to Andre, or even if Andre has left the business in Scott's hands, maybe he's asked this Shawnee to oversee things for him, be the one who shows her face."

"Get hold of Colin and Mason to see if they can find out who she is, where she lives and whatever. We'll need a word with her."

George opened up a new WhatsApp group for their copper and private detective, asking them to get back to him with the details as soon as possible. He popped the phone away and gave Andre's house another once-over. The bloke wasn't short of money—unsurprising when he dealt in drugs. His home was a four-storey Victorian set in a long row opposite more of the same. A set of five steps led up to each front door, wrought-iron fencing with fleur-de-lis on top separating small gardens from the public footpath. Some were decorated with pots of flowers or mini fir trees, whereas others had shingle or artificial grass. It was clearly the type of street where everyone wanted to make a good impression. Individual parking bays lined the road, a few of them empty where people had gone to work.

Last night, after Eddie had done whatever he did with dead bodies, Jet had messaged him to take the bunch of keys found in Scott's pocket to collect an Audi from behind the art gallery, sending him one of the pictures from the surveillance which clearly showed the number plate. Scott had obviously been using Andre's car.

Greg glanced in the rearview mirror. "Jet's here with Pearl."

George and Greg got out of the van and waited for the women on the pavement. Jet emerged from a white Kia (probably stolen) in a black wig, a brown coat with a big fur collar, high heels, and oversized sunglasses.

"Why the fuck have you chosen a disguise that draws attention to you?" George said.

"Good morning to you, too, and the answer to your question is because if someone's caught up in what I look like, if they had to give a description, they're least likely to notice the size of my nose or the shape of my lips when I look like a fucking Italian movie star or a Mafia wife. And if people around here think the latter then they're going to keep their mouths shut. No one wants a horse's head on their pillow, do they."

"Fair enough."

Pearl got out of the car, just as glamorous as Jet. Her long black wig, bright-red lipstick to match her dress and coat, and black high heels, gave the impression she was loaded. She'd gone for large square sunglasses with gold arms, Gucci imprinted on them. He conceded they'd done well. They could be related. And Mafia wives (for fuck's sake).

Jet eyed Andre's house and asked quietly, "Have you seen any movement?"

"Nope, not in his place," George said, "but a few neighbours have left for work. No one paid us any mind."

He'd stuck a decal for CARDIGAN CLEANING SERVICES on the sides of the van, and in a street like this, that type of work being done was probably par for the course, seeing as the residents likely had the money to afford for someone to come in and get the hoover out for them. However, now two glitzy women had turned up, the pretence that George and Greg were cleaners had gone out of the window. Should any neighbours come out to query what they were doing, George would say Jet and Pearl were Andre's relatives who just so happened to arrive at the same time as them.

This was the sort of shit that should have been talked about last night over dinner, but Jet had been in a rush to go home and had said they would work something out off the cuff today. They would need to be on the same page going forward, so George let her know his thoughts regarding the story for the neighbours, and she nodded her approval.

"We have come over from Naples," she said in a really bad Italian accent. "He is our brother. I know he has sisters because we did our research." She smiled, although it could be more of a grimace because that research may not be the truth. "Actually, I'll say we are his cousins. Come on, let's see what this morning will bring us, then."

George and Greg went up the stairs, the women following, all of them putting on latex gloves. He was conscious they looked conspicuous doing that and were bound to draw attention. Greg tapped on the door then rang the bell. With no response, he took keys from Jet who must have got them back from Eddie. George glanced around to see if anyone observed them, but no curtains twitched and no one stood in windows on either side of the road.

An uneasy feeling set up home in his belly. They all filed inside, the women lifting their sunglasses and perching them on their heads. Jet closed the door. They stood in a large square hallway with stairs directly ahead. Everything was done out in white. To the left stood three doors, and on the strips of wall in between, sets of three small photographs in black frames from the lintels to the skirting boards, each artistic image black-and-white shots of London. The floor reminded George of being in a bathroom, white tiles with marble streaks in grey, a carpet runner going up the middle of the stairs in a matching storm-cloud colour. All in all, it was a tasteful place so far.

"Andre?" George called. "It's George and Greg Wilkes doing a welfare check."

No answer.

"We'll spread out," George said, "but remain in pairs. Pearl, you're with me."

She looked to her boss for direction on that one. Jet nodded and jerked her head at Greg for them to go upstairs. With four floors to cover, they needed to get a shift on.

"Stay close to me," George told Pearl.

He opened the first door and popped his head inside first, then entered. It would likely be described as a reception room on Rightmove, or maybe a snug, but to George it was a common or garden living room, albeit a bloody lush one. Nice leather armchairs with a matching sofa, mahogany-coloured to match the built-in TV wall at the end. The black walls and ceiling gave it a sophisticated look, and he imagined it would be like a cinema in here at night with the red velvet curtains closed. While it was interesting to get a bead on Andre's personality that had clearly been injected into this lounge space, the man wasn't here, so it was time to move on.

Behind the next door, a small toilet and sink, and behind the third, an L-shaped kitchen that spanned the width of the house behind the stairs. A wall of bifold doors gave a good view of the paved garden that had an elevated wooden platform at the end with a hot tub beneath a covered gazebo, the cream curtains fluttering in the breeze.

"We're going to have to check that tub, just to be on the safe side," George said.

"What, you think there could be a body in there?"

He looked at Pearl who seemed apprehensive, a far cry from the gun-wielding woman of last night. Maybe her courage deserted her when she wasn't with Jet. Or maybe the fact that she was working alongside The Brothers had properly kicked in and the enormity of the situation had momentarily derailed her, giving her a bit of a wobble.

"We can't rule anything out," he said and smiled to try and give her some reassurance.

But she must have been on jobs like this with Jet. If she was a right-hand woman, she'd have seen all manner of things going on, and it was obvious last night she'd had training in how to fire a gun, not to mention silently asking for permission to do it.

They looked around—the top cupboards held no hidden treasure and the bottom ones were full of crockery. Finding nothing in the drawers, he withdrew the keys from his pocket and opened the bifold doors. He drew them across and stepped outside, heading for the hot tub, checking the patio slabs to see if any of them looked as though they'd been raised and then put back recently. They all appeared uniform, so he shrugged off his uneasy feeling in his gut that a body might be underneath.

With Pearl's help, he unclipped then lifted the lid off the tub. The scent of chlorine wafted up, so someone had been maintaining the water, which was clear, no body floating in it. They secured the lid and returned to the house, locking up. In the hallway, George spotted yet another door, opposite the one for the kitchen, nestled beneath the stairs.

Pearl looked at him. "It could just be where he stores his shoes and things."

"You're right, it could, but I don't like leaving anything to chance."

George opened the door. A slim chain dangled just inside the frame to his right, head height, and he pulled it, switching on a single bulb with no shade. Wooden steps went directly beneath the ones in the house. He went down them, his shoes tapping loudly, echoing, and turned right at the bottom where he determined he was now standing under the area by the front door. Along the wall where the snug window was, a vast wine rack that held at least a thousand bottles from floor to ceiling. He stared the other way towards where the kitchen would be, taking in the fact that two archway walls clearly held up the ceiling.

The first space was obviously for the wine, and George stepped into the second section beyond the first arch, so if anyone sprang out at him he could protect Pearl. On the left- and right-hand walls, built-in cupboards that looked like they could have come from IKEA. He opened a couple to find a wealth of things stored inside as if Andre was afraid of running out. Packs of toilet roll, shower gel, shampoo, deodorant. Pearl helped him check the cupboards on the other side, and those ones had cans of food, drinks, and posh of the poshest, packets of crisps hanging from individual pegs attached to pullout metal strips on the underside of a shelf.

"If we have another pandemic, I know where I'm coming for my shopping," George said.

"Maybe that's why Scott took on Andre's identity. The real bloke's still suffering the effects of lockdown and Scott was doing his job for him so Andre didn't lose face."

"Could be, but what I don't get is why Andre would have picked Scott. He was an absolute pleb."

"Not too much of a pleb because he pulled this off. He did a good Italian accent. Or maybe Scott was forced into it. As you know, some people have no choice in what they do."

She referred to her stint in the boarded-up house, and now was the perfect time for him to talk to her about what had been bugging him ever since he'd seen her last night.

"Is that the case for you now? Do you only work for Jet because you're forced to? Because despite who she is, we can help you with that."

She shook her head. "I appreciate your concern, but I work for her because I went to ask her for a sex-work permit and she offered me a job, it's as simple as that."

"No offence, but as far as I could see when we set you free from the house, you didn't exactly have any knowledge of how to be a right-hand woman, so why would she have picked you?"

"I can't be bothered to take offence at that, but if you must know, she said she saw something in me, and also that teaching someone from scratch was better for her because I hadn't had time to develop bad habits. Basically, I landed on my feet and I'm trying to move on."

"Which means you don't want me asking questions about your past."

"That would be about right. I don't feel the need to go into it. I am who I am now, and that's all that matters. Come on, let's check the next section."

He had a feeling she'd been hurt in the past, more than what he knew. Why else would she want to forget it all? He'd offer her therapy with Vic, but it wasn't his place, and besides, she'd probably bite his head off for making such a suggestion.

They moved beneath the second arch and into a gym. State-of-the-art equipment had been placed with enough space between each item that it didn't appear cramped. George got another insight into how well-off Andre was. A lot of this stuff would have cost a fortune. A long red punchbag hung from the ceiling on a chain, and again George got pandemic vibes, imagining Andre using this space to centre his mind, maybe to stop him from going stir crazy. Another punchbag lay on the floor beside an expensive treadmill, although it wasn't as packed out as the other one. It looked as though the stuffing had been smacked so often the bag had gone misshapen. This one was a different brand to the red one, and it was black. Something about it wasn't right, so George went closer, crouching to get a better look.

"Is it just me, or are there splashes of something dark on this bag?"

Pearl came to have a nose. "They might only seem dark because the bag's black."

"Hmm." George got up and moved round the other side, finding a zip. He pushed the bag over a bit so the zip was now facing upwards, then he pulled it down and frowned at the contents. It wasn't stuffing or polystyrene beads as he'd expected. His guts rolled over. He stared at something wrapped up in what he could only describe as layers and layers of clingfilm.

"What the fucking hell?" Pearl whispered, a trembling hand rising to her mouth.

George took his keys out of his pocket, glad he had a Swiss army knife on the bunch. He selected one of the blades and carefully cut a four-inch slice through the layers.

The stench of old death.

He recoiled, pressing the back of his wrist beneath his nose. "Fuck, we've either found Andre or someone other poor fucker. It's best we leave him in the bag and move the body elsewhere to see if we can identify it."

"But it's daylight. We'll get seen."

"As far as anyone's concerned in this street, me and my brother are cleaners. Us carrying that bag out inside a rug probably won't be taken any notice of. We'd best let Greg and Jet know what we've found. The sooner we get the body out of here the better."

George zipped up the punchbag, his mind full of the possible scenario that had taken place here. Had Scott and Andre had an argument? Had it gone wrong and Scott ended up killing Andre—or whoever else this was? Scott had never struck George as someone who'd know where to go and bury a body without getting caught, but it was a genius idea to wrap the corpse up tight so not much smell escaped, or fluid, as was placing it in an empty punchbag.

Had Scott and this Shawnee woman lived here the whole time the body was decomposing? If not, Scott must at least have come to the house on some occasions, otherwise he wouldn't have been captured in photographs taken by Jet's surveillance men. Another thought sauntered into George's head. What if Andre was the killer and he'd absconded? What if Scott had been here when the murder had happened and he'd bribed Andre into letting him assume his identity?

Nah, Scott wasn't that clever.

They were going to have to be careful when they carried the body out now that George had made a slit in the clingfilm. Depending on how long the body had been here, there might be leakage that would seep through the slit, then the zip, and onto the rug before they'd had a chance to put it in the van.

They went back up to the hallway. Greg and Jet were just coming downstairs.

"There's a lot of Scott's stuff up in the main bedroom," Greg said. "His passport and whatever. We've gathered it up so we can burn it later. There's stuff belonging to a woman, too.

I've explained to Jet about Shawnee and who she might be."

That seemed to go over Pearl's head, as though she was so fixated on what was in the punchbag that she hadn't taken in that a woman was also involved in this mess.

"We found a bit more than that," George said. "There's a body that's been wrapped in clingfilm or whatever the fuck it is. It's been put inside a punchbag. I can only assume the original stuffing was removed. There's another punchbag hanging from the ceiling, and it looks newer."

Jet sighed. "If the body belongs to Andre, Scott must have continued with all of his usual customers, probably working with them like he did with me via the phone, keeping visits to a minimum. I wonder what he thought when I insisted we have a face-to-face meeting before I committed to buying from him?"

"I doubt he was bothered because he certainly looks similar enough get away with it," George said. "Only we turned up and ruined everything for him. Right, because this happened on Cardigan, we'll take responsibility for disposing of the body and having a word with Shawnee."

"The body might be too far gone that we can't work out who it is," Greg said. "Andre could be off somewhere else, alive and kicking, and some other poor bastard's inside that clingfilm, their family none the wiser."

"There's only one way to find out," George said. "We need a rug to wrap it in."

Jet massaged her temples. "We'll come with you if you don't mind. I feel like we need to see this through to the end."

George nodded and went off to find a rug.

Chapter Nine

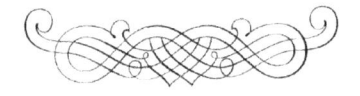

Pearl had sensed George wanted to ask her a shedload of questions about what she'd been up to since she'd been rescued. She hoped he wouldn't bring the subject up again as she didn't feel the need to explain anything to him—nor could she be bothered to do so. She lived and worked on the Proust Estate, and while all the bullshit with Mocha had happened on Cardigan, she'd given her statement to the police about her abduction, the goings-on in that house, and the night she'd been granted freedom. She wasn't going to go to the police and tell them she now knew who the rescuers were. She assumed Greg had been with George, but she had no clue who the other two men were and didn't want to know either. When she'd walked out of the police station, that had been it for her, a full stop at the end of another snippet of her life.

She glanced at Jet where they stood in the hallway. Greg had gone off after George, she assumed to find a rug.

"Show me where the body is," Jet said.

Pearl led the way downstairs, going straight to the gym at the end. She pointed at the bag on the floor. "It's in there."

"How are you feeling?"

That was the thing with Jet, she cared about Pearl's well-being which was more than could be said for so many people who'd lived in her life. Pearl appreciated being cared for and smiled at her boss.

"I kind of had a feeling we were going to find a body here today but I told myself it was just my imagination running away with me, so then when George opened the bag and I saw the clingfilm…" Pearl swallowed acid that had shot up into the back of her throat. "Anyway, I know I've seen stuff while working with you, but I haven't been so up close and personal with it. I've been on the sidelines. I shot Scott last night, and even though I knew I wasn't going to kill him, I can't get over how easily I pulled the trigger. There was no remorse or anything, I just wanted to get the job done to show you I could do it. And then when George cut the clingfilm… I hoped it would be full of drugs or something, you know? And I wasn't prepared."

"For what?"

"For not actually being bothered that it was a body. I think something broke inside me when I was in that house."

"From what you've told me about your life, something broke inside you long before you were abducted, maybe even as far back as a little kid. What I think is going on is your mind can't take any more trauma, so it's trivialising things to keep you sane. Been there, done that. It really isn't so bad once you get used to feeling detached. It's quite nice not to have your emotions all over the place." Jet crouched and undid the zip. She leaned in close to look through the slit. "Either that eyeball has dissolved as the body's been rotting or it was removed by whoever killed this person." She pulled the zip up and stood.

"It's bound to be Andre, isn't it?"

"I would imagine so."

"Who's Shawnee? Is it someone we should be worried about?"

"I don't know yet, but we'll get to the bottom of it. She's been paying Andre's protection money to the twins' man."

"How long for?"

"Months."

"Bloody hell, so if she isn't Andre's girlfriend and she's been in on this with Scott, then it's been going on for a bloody long time."

"Or she *was* Andre's girlfriend and decided to get into bed with Scott."

"Can you look into this yourself?"

"Ordinarily I would have to leave it to the twins because it's their patch, but because we were involved in this prior to them coming along and opening our eyes, yes, we can have a poke around, but I need to let them know my intentions first."

"Your intention to do what?" George asked, carrying one end of a large rug.

Jet explained what they'd been talking about.

"Yeah," George said, "if we've all got our people looking into it then it'll be resolved quicker. Hang on, let me check my phone to see if our copper or the private detective have got back to me."

He put the rug down, leaving Greg holding the other end, and took his phone out. He prodded the screen a few times, nodding to himself.

"Our copper's having a little moan because he doesn't like looking at the database for small things like this—he hates using someone else's username to log in and worries he'll get caught. Anyway, he's come through. Shawnee Devonshire, age twenty-five, current address down as nineteen Foxton Avenue—it sounds posh but it really isn't. She's a council estate girl."

"Nothing wrong with that," Pearl said.

"There isn't," George said, "and what I was getting at with that statement was that we're not dealing with some posh totty here, we've likely got someone who knows how to claw her way up to the top."

Pearl wasn't sure whether he was making a dig at her, but if he was, did it even matter that he'd hit the nail on the head? *She* was someone who knew how to claw her way up. She had wanted to be someone important for as long as she could remember. At first it had been being an important person to her mum, and when that was no longer on the table she wanted the importance in different ways. She needed to know her existence was for a reason, and if it meant earning money, enough to buy herself a house one day, then she'd have amounted to something in her own eyes. She'd have become so much more than what her mother had engineered her to be.

"What's the plan now then?" Jet asked.

"We take the body to our warehouse—Pearl, you must never tell anyone the location of it."

She tutted. "I know the rules."

"Good. Then we can either unpack the body to see who it is or go and pay Shawnee a visit in Foxton, assuming she's home. We'll get surveillance outside this place just in case she comes back while we're gone. I'll send a message to arrange that now." He jabbed at his screen.

"What if me and Pearl go and visit Shawnee while you take the body to the warehouse?" Jet suggested. "She'll probably be more receptive speaking to two women. Four people in a group might appear intimidating, and she could clam up."

George looked up from the screen and nodded. "Good idea. Right, one of our blokes is coming over to do surveillance here and another is going over to Foxton to keep an eye out before you get there. What's your plan if she's home?"

"Ask her if we can have a chat about Andre and Scott."

"And if she doesn't want to?"

"We'll let you know and wait for you to arrive. I'm sure she'll be more open to her own leaders than she will with me—not that I plan to tell her who I really am." Jet smirked. "I might just have fun and pretend I'm Italian Mafia."

"You two leave now," George said, "otherwise it's going to look weird with all four of us leaving the house with the rug. Say something loudly out the front as if you're speaking to Andre inside the house. You know the drill in case a neighbour's watching and listening."

"I'll be in touch."

Jet led the way upstairs, and Pearl lowered her sunglasses in preparation for going outside.

Nerves tickled her belly, but the excited kind where she didn't know what to expect. A crowd of neighbours could have gathered out there in their absence, waiting to ask questions as soon as someone opened the front door. Then again, the surveillance men had reported that this street was relatively quiet, so maybe there was nothing to be worried about.

Nevertheless, when they were out on the top step, Jet kept her head down while she put her sunglasses back on then went into action, leaning back inside and calling out, "See you later, Andre darling! Love you!"

She closed the door, and they navigated the steps, Pearl's heart thudding along with her footsteps down the garden path. Jet left the gate ajar, probably to make things easier for the twins, then got in the driver's seat of the Kia, Pearl hurrying around the front of the vehicle to get in the passenger side. They put their seat belts on, and Jet drove away, waving at Andre's house as they passed.

No neighbours were in sight, and Pearl let out a deep breath. As usual when they were out on a job and had a moment, they sat in quiet contemplation for a while to absorb what had gone on. Jet had taught Pearl to do that, saying it was good to cement things in your mind prior to moving to the next job or location, a period of adjustment she felt was essential. Sometimes, though, that time wasn't available, and at the end of the days where they'd rushed from one thing to another, Pearl had found herself exhausted. She completely understood the bandwidth Jet spoke about.

Pearl had only been working for her for a few short weeks, but it honestly felt like much longer than that. Going by her past experiences, each section she had lived in, she had settled into them as though that was all she'd ever known. That wasn't normal, was it, to jump from one section to another so quickly and effortlessly? How many more phases of her life would she dive into, or was this it now, her life with Jet the last transition? Surely not. Wouldn't there be a man, kids, and a couple of puppies in her future?

Ten minutes passed, then Jet spoke. "Okay, so I've been having a think on how to play this. For all we know, this Shawnee might know what Andre's sisters look like, so we can't say we're related to him in that way, but like I said to George, we can pretend to be cousins. We've come over on a visit from Italy. Going by her reaction, we'll be able to gauge what the hell's been going on—as in, whether she looks guilty or not."

"She might not knowingly have anything to do with it all. What if she was employed by who she thought was Andre when it was really Scott? She could be innocent."

"Then why tell the twins' man that she was Andre's girlfriend?"

"Oh, you didn't tell me that bit. So what are we doing after we've made out we're his cousins?"

"The aim is to get her to ask us in. I'll message the twins to let them know they can turn up and do what they've got to do, which is likely taking her off to interrogate her, the same sort of thing as I would do."

"Okay."

The satnav announced that Foxton Avenue was coming up on the left. Jet took the turning and drove slowly while they both took a side of the road and looked for the correct house. Pearl spotted number nineteen and pointed it out. Jet parked, and once again they took a minute or two to sit in silence, both of them scoping out the street but especially Shawnee's address. All the houses looked the same, the front doors identical and a boring white. The double-glazed windows reflected the clouds opposite with the sun peeking out from behind, which obscured any view they'd have had to see somebody watching them from behind the glass.

"Ready?" Jet asked.

Pearl nodded. This sort of thing was something she was well used to now, a little visit where they pretended to be people they weren't just to get information so they could form a bigger picture. Between them they had many wigs and pairs of sunglasses, and Jet was right when she'd said to George that people were more receptive to two women than they were a group. It had been proven time and again when Jet and Pearl had been out on their own compared to when they took some of the men with them.

They got out of the car. The sun went behind the clouds, and it was like a light had gone off, removing the reflection from the windows. Pearl could now see Venetian blinds at Shawnee's windows, the slats open, although she couldn't see anything beyond the slitted spaces. She didn't get the sense they were being watched as they walked up the garden path, but that didn't mean they weren't. Jet pressed the bell button, and they waited.

A black woman with a short Afro appeared, her eyebrows shaped to give the impression she was in perpetual surprise. Her makeup was as perfect as Pearl's and Jet's. Her crop top and low-rise jeans revealed a toned stomach and an innie belly button.

"Can I help you?" she asked.

"Sorry to trouble you," Jet said, in full Italian mode, "but are you Shawnee?"

"Yes. Who's asking?"

"Our cousin told us where you live just in case we needed to contact anyone in an emergency."

"What's the emergency and who's your cousin?"

"Andre Alexander. He is not at home and has not been answering his phone. We have come over from Italy as a surprise, we arrived two days ago, and each time we have been to his house, no one has been there."

"That's weird, because he was there last night. Well, I say last night, it was about six after I'd finished doing the cleaning."

"You are his girlfriend, yes?"

"Err, no, I'm the cleaner."

"So why would he say you were a girlfriend?"

"Because that's what he told people to stop them asking questions. Some of them along his row are so *nosy*."

"So you pretend to be his girlfriend... Okay, so why would he give us your address?"

"I have no idea. I'd have thought his sisters would have been his emergency contact."

"You say you saw him about six. Did he say where he was going?"

"He did as it happened. He was off to an art gallery. Look, to save us standing out here and the neighbours getting an eyeful, do you want to come in for a cuppa? I've got an hour before I have to go out. I can give Andre a ring for you and see where he is, although I don't understand why he wouldn't answer the phone to you."

"We do not understand either," Jet said.

Shawnee turned her back and walked down the hallway. Jet and Pearl stepped inside, the pair of them lifting their sunglasses onto their heads and following the woman into a kitchen. Either she was seriously good at being a billy bullshitter or she was telling the truth. Jet would soon find out, she was good at using a few well-chosen words to catch people out in lies.

"Take a pew at the table. Do you want tea or coffee, or I've got cold drinks in the fridge?"

"Coffee would be lovely," Jet said.

In the past, if they'd had a drink in a place they didn't want to leave their DNA in, they usually took the cups with them. Pearl copped on that they still had the latex gloves on from Andre's house—fucking hell!—and she wiggled her hand at Jet to let her know while Shawnee's back was turned. Jet put her hands on her lap under cover of the table so the gloves were hidden, and Pearl did the same, but if Shawnee hadn't seen them yet then she would when they reached out to take their cups. Unless Jet had no intention of drinking the coffee…

With the kettle on to boil and three cups out on the side, Shawnee went to the fridge to take the milk out, saying, "Do you think something's happened to Andre?"

"If you say you saw him at six, then that is less worrying than us thinking he has been missing for a couple of days. Do you know what he was going to the art gallery for?"

"To sign off on a deal."

"What kind of deal?"

Shawnee poured milk into the cups. "I have no idea."

"So he doesn't confide in you?" Jet asked.

"No, I just clean for him. Oh, and he leaves me money on the worktop to pay the twins' man every Friday."

"The twins' man? Who is this?"

"Ah, you probably don't know about the leaders in London if you've come from Italy. There are two men who look after businesses and whatever. You have to pay them so that they look after you, too."

"Like the Mafia?"

Shawnee laughed and lifted the boiled kettle which had just clicked off. "Err, sort of."

"So you run a cleaning business. Do you pay them protection money to be looked after?"

Shawnee added spoonfuls of coffee to the water.

"It would be dangerous if you didn't, no?" Jet pushed.

"Hmm."

Shawnee handed the cups out, clearly wanting the floor to swallow her up. They'd strayed into dangerous conversation territory, where Jet was possibly on the verge of finding out whether this woman was on the level or not. Surely if she paid protection money for her own business, the man who collected it would have recognised her at Andre's. Maybe this was something that needed to be passed on to the twins. If she *wasn't* paying them protection cash, then they ought to know about it.

Shawnee sat at the table with them and took a phone out of her jeans pocket. "I'll give Andre a ring now." She fiddled with her screen and then put it on speakerphone, frowning as it rang and rang. "Oh, he's not answering me either."

"Let me just try him again myself." Jet took her mobile out but didn't bother with speakerphone.

She'll be ringing the twins.

"It's sent me to voicemail." Jet paused. "Andre, we are at Shawnee's, your emergency contact. You did not say she is your cleaning lady… We are confused about what is going on. Please could you contact us?" She ended the call. "Hopefully we will hear something soon." Then she launched into a conversation about the crappy weather in London compared to Italy, all to pass the time until either the twins arrived or she felt it was the right time to exit.

Chapter Ten

The new doctor on Ward F, Hilary Thompson, stern-faced and red-haired, sat opposite Miranda in one of the 'chatting' rooms that was supposed to put everyone at ease—nice wallpaper with flamingos standing on one leg all over it, comfy leather armchairs, a pink fluffy rug. She offered one of those smiles Miranda hated, the type that showed she pitied her, but not in a good way. The pity didn't come from a nice place but from that nugget of spite inside a person who thought they were better than the people they were dealing with. Superior. Miranda was going to miss the other doctor who'd gone on maternity leave ("Please call me Charlene, Dr Greene is so formal, and we're all friends here."). At least she gave a proper shit. At least she looked at you with concern.

"Why are you here?" Thompson asked somewhat abruptly after introducing herself in a bored monotone.

It had been asked in such an offhand way that Miranda didn't want to reply, didn't want to give the woman the time of day, but if she didn't toe the line it would be a black mark against her. "Drug-induced psychosis."

"And this occurred because…"

Miranda could really do with Thompson reading all of her notes before asking these questions—then there'd be no need to ask them. Or maybe she was being evaluated. Her release date might depend on how she responded. If she expressed how sorry she was for her behaviour, if she acted like she wasn't insane, maybe she'd be let out early. After all, she'd followed the rules here, had taken the medication, proving she wanted to get better.

Miranda took a deep breath. "I hate what happened and will always feel guilty about it. I had a bit too much cocaine and marijuana in the same bender session—I'd never taken drugs before, hadn't even drunk that much alcohol until then. Something bad had happened, and I just wanted to forget. Anyway, when I left the Blue Dolphin, that's the pub I was in, I hallucinated and thought a woman was attacking me when all she wanted to do was help—I'd apparently stumbled, and she'd tried to catch me. She had her hands out as she was coming towards me, and I was convinced I was going to be strangled. To be fair, she did look like a demon. I realise now that it was the drugs and my mind playing tricks on me. I lashed out at her, got arrested, got assessed, and because of my mental health issues from before, I was detained here on a section three for up to six months."

And what an experience it had been so far. Miranda had made a few friends who'd come and gone, but two of the originals remained. Then there were the outright nutters, the ones who stayed here for a year at a time, maybe even longer. If she hadn't attacked that woman, she might not have been placed here, but coupled with the shit that had gone on before Mum died, she hadn't really stood much chance.

They thought she was crazy because of her suicide attempt. Nice.

"What were your mental health issues from before?" Thompson asked.

Here we go. Time to reel it all off. *"My dad left before I was born which meant my mum had to bring me up on her own. We lived on a council estate in a rough street. Mum was on benefits for the most part, but she got cash in hand for having men in."*

Thompson raised her eyebrows. She clearly wanted Miranda to spell it out.

Fuck's sake.

"She was a prostitute, and then I was a prostitute."

"From what age?"

"Sixteen. Sometimes men had a go with me after they'd been with my mum, other times they came to see me specifically, but she took the money they paid for me. At the end of the week she gave me my wages of fifty quid."

"How did you feel about this?"

How do you think I fucking felt? *"It messed with my head, all of it. I got a bit depressed and ended up going to the doctor who put me on tablets. They made me feel worse, so I stopped taking them but carried on getting the prescriptions. On my eighteenth birthday, I swallowed three packets in one go and thought I'd closed my eyes for the last time, but I wasn't that lucky. Mum found me and rang an ambulance. They were going to put me in here then, but I got away with it for some reason."*

Thompson's look of pity had changed to mild curiosity. "Did you tell anyone back then what your mother was forcing you to do?"

"No."

"What happened after you were released from hospital?"

"I had to see a psychiatrist. She signed me off after my block of free sessions had ended. She said I needed more but I'd have to pay for them, and I couldn't afford it, three hundred quid a go, so…"

"What was the bad news you received that meant you took cocaine and marijuana?"

"My mum died. It was the day of her funeral."

"I'm sorry to hear that."

"She was murdered in our house."

"How do you feel about that?"

"On the one hand I loved her because she was my mum, but on the other I hated her because she was my mum, do you see what I mean?"

"I can understand that, yes. You said hated, past tense… Do you no longer hate her?"

"No, she was a victim of circumstance." Miranda did *still hate ger guts, but she wasn't going to admit it. If she'd 'forgiven' her mother, it would go in her favour.*

"Now that some time has passed, what are your thoughts on your life prior to coming here?"

"I'm ready to go back to the house, despite what happened there. The sex, the murder."

"Are there any other family members who could help you when you go back home?"

"No, it was always just me and her." And the men. So many men.

"Do you know who your father is? Could he help?"

"No and no." Please let me out. Please don't make me stay here.

Oddly, Thompson switched subjects to the weather, mentioning how nice it had been on her walk to the hospital today. "A bit of sunshine works wonders when you open the curtains and see it in the morning, doesn't it."

"I wouldn't know, my window faces a brick wall."

It was called Ward F but was actually a three-storey building situated beside the main hospital, built eighteen years ago. She suspected it was to keep the mega nutbags contained so there was no chance of them escaping into other parts of the hospital and hurting someone. Ward F was always locked up, and only a member of staff could open the doors. What was scary was that people like Miranda shouldn't be placed on the same floor as those who had a tendency to stab the shit out of someone because the voices in their head told them to do it, but on paper it appeared she was exactly like them, except she'd wanted to do harm because of psychosis and the very real feelings of needing to defend herself. Voices hadn't come into it.

Thompson had switched subjects again. Miranda told herself off for not paying attention. Showing signs of drifting, of not listening, wasn't going to put her in a good light.

"Going by Dr Greene's final assessment of you prior to her leaving, she feels the full length of your detention here wasn't actually necessary. A month or so would have been enough, in her opinion. As you can appreciate, I need to read up on everybody here and determine if any early releases are imminent based on my interactions with you all."

"How long will that take?"

"It will take as long as it takes." Thompson drew a finger down a page of Miranda's file. "I see you have things squared away with the council for now, they've agreed to let you keep the house, so I don't understand

what you're worrying about there—it states here that you've been fretting about it recently."

You clearly haven't read on to see what happens if I'm stuck here for longer than six months, you stupid fucking cow.

Miranda smiled despite wanting to scream.

Dismissed, she left and made her way to the common room on floor two, not floor three where her bedroom was. She'd rather sit with her two friends who weren't outright crackers. The ones on her level were a bit scary sometimes, and she wasn't in the mood to walk on eggshells and keep looking over her shoulder.

Nurse Nora gave her a smile as Miranda approached the desk in the reception area. "All done?"

"Yeah."

"What did you think of her?"

Miranda wasn't going to tell the truth. She needed to get out, get home, and if she slagged Thompson off, Nora might go and tell her. She liked to gossip. "She was nice."

Nora appeared let down. "Good. Are you off up to your room now?"

"No, I'm going for a chat."

Miranda wandered into the common room, ignoring the majority of those present, and went to sit with Alicia, a nineteen-year-old with bipolar, and

Valerie, a sixty-something. Whatever Val was in here for she wouldn't say. Miranda had been open with these two, revealing everything, and it had been nice to spend time with people who didn't judge her and actually said it was no wonder she'd tried to end it all, considering the life she'd been forced to live.

If Miranda had been told about some woman's life—hers—she'd have understood why she'd tried to end it, too. She hadn't exactly had the best upbringing. Not only had she grown up seeing men come and go, but as soon as she was old enough to use the washing machine, she'd been on laundry duty. Then it had moved on to the whole house duty, which had become her responsibility to clean, something she'd struggled to do once she was in secondary school and had to study.

It had all been a bit shit really.

"How did it go with Thompson?" Alicia asked. "I've been dreading seeing her all morning."

"I won't sugarcoat it. She looked down her nose at me and basically told me I'm stuck here until she decides I can go." That wasn't true, Miranda could apply to discharge herself, but with Thompson in the driving seat, the outcome likely wouldn't be what Miranda wanted. Why put herself through all that for the same result?

Val sighed. "And it's not like you've got any family who can back you up in being discharged either, is it. You're not even mad, you just made a mistake while coked off your tits."

"I agreed to stay here for as long as I need to because that's what Charlene suggested, that it would be in my best interests to see this through, but I'm honestly thinking about looking into discharging myself. I'm worried about losing the house. The six months is coming up…"

Because she'd been detained and had people poking into her life and circumstances, she'd had to reveal her living arrangements. The mental health social worker had been brought in, and the issue of the house being empty had come up. According to the rules, as a council tenant she was allowed to be away from home for up to six weeks in one stretch or eight weeks in a whole year without having to tell anyone, so when she'd found out she'd been placed in here for up to six months, the social worker had gone to bat for her, telling the council Miranda was in hospital.

Miranda had received a letter to say that if she had to remain here any longer than six months then her case would be reviewed. There was a possibility she'd lose her home. It wasn't as if she could ask someone to live there for a while either because the council had warned her it would be classed as subletting.

Not that I even have anyone to ask.

"Thompson said she's got to review everybody's cases before she can move forward," Miranda said.

"But I'm due to leave here tomorrow." Val drummed her fingertips on the wooden arm of her chair, her expression thunderous.

"You can't be included in that, surely," Alicia said. "You've already been signed off by Charlene to go home."

"There had better not be an issue or I'm going to seriously kick off." Val stared into the middle distance. "These past six months have dragged on forever."

But at least Val had family visiting her every other day during that time. Miranda had no one, not even Bunty—she hadn't told her neighbour where she'd gone. And there were no friends. As soon as she'd left school, her mates had lost contact—accidentally on purpose? She didn't know and hadn't bothered to reach out to them in case they told her to fuck off. For all she knew, they'd just tolerated her at school, glad to be rid of her when they'd all parted ways.

"If you kick off then you might have to stay longer," Alicia reminded Val quietly.

"True." Val folded her arms.

Miranda narrowed her eyes. "I reckon Thompson's doing all these interviews because she's got a God complex. She basically said she wasn't taking Charlene's word for it on who we are and she'd make her own mind up. Fair enough, I get that, but what if she doesn't see us like Charlene does?"

"There are fifty-odd people in Ward F," Alicia said. "It's going to take her ages to get to know us all, but like I just said, there's no way she should be allowed to fuck about with any release orders that have already been signed off before she came here."

"I just want her to let me out of here," Miranda said. "I want the chance to start again."

Jesus Christ, it wasn't too much to ask, was it?

Chapter Eleven

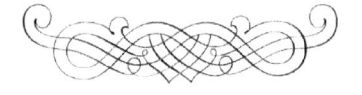

If Shawnee played her cards right, she'd get out of this spot of bother without any trouble—but what if she didn't hold the ace and everything came tumbling down? She'd known, ever since she'd become Andre's cleaner, that she wasn't going to be a trustworthy person when it came to him. He had a beautiful house, and it was clear he had a lot of money—money she wanted. Over the months, she'd been exposed to phone calls he'd had where he'd chatted away as though she wasn't there with her feather duster, and it became completely clear what he was selling, and it wasn't a pretty garden. He was no landscape artist like he'd claimed to the neighbours. When he'd gone out, she'd nosed around his house, trying to find the drugs he'd mentioned to whoever he'd been speaking to. She'd discovered them down in the cellar, bricks of cocaine hidden behind toilet rolls and cans and God knew what else in the cupboards.

She'd learned he had people who came to collect those bricks. Buyers. She'd also learned how he'd run his business. Watched him putting PIN codes on his phone, and she'd memorised them. He thought she was just a cleaner doing her job, and once, he'd asked her if she knew what he was really up to. She'd shrugged and said it was none of her business, she was employed to clean and that was the end of it.

He'd never asked her to give Martin the protection money, that had come later after Andre had died. Since convincing Scott to work with her on this scam, she'd wondered whether the time would come when things would go tits up. Andre's sisters had been in contact over texts at various points, and Shawnee or Scott had responded so they thought Andre was still alive, but Shawnee had never heard about any cousins. Still, the proof they existed was sitting right in front of her, but within the next half an hour she'd get rid of them and warn Scott they'd have to be a bit more careful. As in limiting the amount of time they spent in Andre's house now that family members had come poking around. Granted, it was a lovely place, and she'd enjoyed pretending it was hers, but really, she ought to just go there for when Martin collected the protection money.

Scott had become Andre, dealing with the drug deliveries, handing them out when people came to collect, always with his sunglasses on, but they really did need to watch what they were doing now.

The body. They were going to have to get rid of it.

The problem was, neither of them knew where to put it, hence why it was wrapped in clingfilm and hidden in the punchbag. Thank God for Andre's obsessive habit of ordering far too much of everything, otherwise they'd never have had enough to wrap him up. In recent months, they'd very rarely left his house, stocking up on everything they needed via Amazon so they didn't have to nip to the shops much—all paid for on Andre's bank card. The least they were seen, the better she felt.

During her time watching Andre, she'd learned every single one of his passwords, and PIN codes for his banking apps, so she was fully aware of how much money they had to play with. On the day he'd died, he'd had half a million in his account; the funds appeared legitimate, but they most certainly weren't. He supposedly ran a garden renovation business, which accounted for the large amounts of money being paid in by customers—and they *were* customers, but they paid for drugs not landscaping. The mortgage and bills got paid every month on direct debit, and it was as if Andre still lived. Everything had remained exactly the same apart from no face-to-face meetings with new customers anymore.

Until that bitch from the Proust Estate had insisted on one. They'd never have agreed to it if the transaction wasn't so big, if the profit they'd make from it wasn't so eye-popping.

It was a bit worrying that Scott wasn't answering his phone—or Andre's. Had something happened at the art gallery? Scott had perfected an Italian accent, he'd had enough months to practise it as well as Andre's mannerisms (Shawnee had recorded Andre on one occasion using a tiny camera hidden behind a vase so Scott could study the footage). Had Scott mucked up somehow? Had Jet Proust asked him questions about Andre that he hadn't been able to answer? Was she the type of woman to contact his family abroad to get some information on him only they would know?

And the biggest question of all, should Shawnee contact Jet to find out if she knew where he was?

"How long have you been Andre's cleaner?" The older of the women lowered her sunglasses onto her nose, which was a little odd. Maybe she suffered from migraines?

She'd slipped it in earlier that her name was Vittoria and the other was Aurora. Shawnee didn't like it that the conversation had moved from general things back to stuff she didn't want to talk about. She was going to have to be vague.

"Months. I can't remember when I first started."

"You must keep good records, no?" Aurora asked. "Maybe you could check them."

Aurora had barely spoken, Vittoria taking the lead, so why she was piping up now? And why would they need the exact date Shawnee had started working for Andre? It was still bugging her why he'd even given his cousins her address. What the chuff was that all about?

"You would need the records for proving to those leaders when you should start paying this protection money you told us about."

"That is right," Vittoria said, "you would not want to anger the leaders."

Shawnee wasn't about to admit that she didn't pay the fucking leaders a penny and didn't see why she should. She could look after herself, thanks very much, and didn't need the twins on hand. Anyway, it would be like phoning the police if she needed their help. It'd take them ages to get to her, so she'd take her chances by herself. Anyway, who did she need protecting from? Someone who wanted to steal her mop and bucket? Not that she used those anymore. She hadn't been a cleaner ever since she'd been living off Andre's money. Why make a wage yourself when someone else's bank account provided it for you?

These women had started to irritate her, and she wanted them gone.

"Do you have a phone number I can have to let you know when Andre gets in contact with me again?" Shawnee asked.

Vittoria nodded and recited a number which Shawnee scribbled down on a pad.

"Do you have a key to his house?" Vittoria asked.

Shawnee's stomach rolled over. These questions were getting a bit too intrusive now. Yes, she understood they must be worried about their cousin, but for fuck's sake. "What?"

"Do you have a key to his house so you can let yourself in to do the cleaning when he is not there?"

Shawnee had to think fast on how to answer this. If she said she had a key, they might ask to borrow it and could potentially find the body if they went snooping. "No, he's always there when I'm due round."

"What days do you clean?"

"Mondays and Fridays." They were drug drop-off and pick-up days, and Martin came on a Friday.

"Does he stay while you are there?"

"Sometimes on a Monday, but Fridays he lets me in then goes out but always leaves the protection money for me to hand over to Martin—that's the leaders' collection man."

"He must trust you if he is letting you do that."

Shawnee shrugged. "I suppose so, but I've never given him any reason *not* to trust me so…"

Vittoria's phone bleeped. She read a message on her screen and nodded to herself, then she showed Aurora who took the phone, read whatever was on it, and handed it back.

Why are they wearing those sorts of gloves? What the fucking hell's going on here?

The cousins stood.

"We will leave you alone now," Vittoria said. "Thank you for the coffee."

Shawnee looked down at the cups. They hadn't even drunk it. Was it because they were used to the posh Italian stuff and didn't like instant?

"Nice gloves," Shawnee said, needing a reaction that would give her an inkling as to why they even had them on.

Vittoria tittered. "Ah, we have had treatment this morning in one of the lovely spas here. These gloves help to keep the moisture in after our manicures."

That was plausible, Shawnee had had it done herself once when she'd had new nails put on, although she'd been told to take the gloves off before she'd left the salon, otherwise the tips of her fingers would have been like prunes. Still, what the hell did she care as to whether the women's fingertips went funny?

Shawnee went first down the hallway, opening the front door, desperate to get rid of them so she could find out what the hell had happened to Scott. Aurora lowered her sunglasses, and the pair said their goodbyes. Nervous that Andre's life had encroached on hers in such a personal way by the women visiting her house, Shawnee shut the door and went into the living room, closing the blind slats enough that she wouldn't be seen watching but she could still see outside. Vittoria and Aurora got in a white car and sat there staring through the windscreen.

They didn't appear to be talking, so what the fuck were they *doing*?

Piss off. Go on, drive away.

Shawnee took her phone out of her pocket and phoned Scott again on Andre's number and, getting no response, she rang Scott's mobile. No answer. She'd already saved Jet Proust's number before Scott had left to go to the art gallery, never dreaming she'd actually need to use it, but if she wanted answers, it looked like she was going to have to.

Using a burner so she could ditch the SIM after the call, she dialled. Stared outside while it rang. Vittoria lifted a phone to her ear, and the ringing stopped.

"Hello?" a woman said in a London accent at the same time Vittoria's lips moved.

Shit. Shit! Could that just be a coincidence? If it wasn't, what the fuck was the Proust leader doing coming here and pretending to be Andre's cousin? Shawnee was going to disguise her voice just in case. A posh accent should do it.

"Um, hello, you don't know me, but I'm Andre Alexander's girlfriend, and I was wondering if you could help me. He said he was meeting you last night for business, but he didn't come home afterwards. Did he happen to tell you where he'd be going, because it's unusual for him not to let me know? I'm extremely worried and I'm thinking of telephoning the police."

"Firstly, how do I know you're really his girlfriend?" Vittoria's lips had moved again.

Jesus Christ.

Shawnee let out a tittering laugh. "I'm not quite sure how I'm supposed to prove it because we're on the phone and I don't have the ability to do FaceTime."

"I meant verbal proof."

"Like…?"

"Tell me what the business meeting was about."

"Landscaping," Shawnee said. "That's what he does, he designs gardens."

"How did you get my number?"

"He gave it to me before he left."

"What for?"

"Now that I think about it, what he said was a bit strange. He said I needed the number in case something happened to him and you would know what it was." *What the hell did I say that for?*

"Didn't you ask why he'd say something like that if he was just meeting me to chat shit about doing up my garden? Did you not think to perhaps phone the police as soon as he didn't come home? I mean, if I had a bloke and he told me something so weird before he left the house, I'd be shitting bricks."

"I couldn't phone the police because of who you are."

"And who am I?"

"Jet Proust, one of the leaders."

"So he told you. What if I'm not?"

"I don't understand why he'd tell me you were if you weren't." This conversation was going in the completely wrong direction. "*Do* you know why my boyfriend didn't come home last night? I understand that I probably have to keep my mouth shut that he even met you, but I'd still like to know."

"I don't know who you think you've been shagging, lady, but it isn't Andre Alexander."

Fuck. "Excuse me?"

"The man who met me was Scott Talbert. I think you might have had the wool pulled over your eyes. You won't be seeing Scott again."

Shawnee pressed the red icon on her screen to end the call, all the while watching Vittoria lower her phone into her lap. She talked to Aurora, although it was obvious now that Vittoria was Jet and the other one was someone called Pearl. Shawnee and Scott had done their homework before he'd gone to the art gallery; not many people had wanted to talk about the leader when they'd been asked, but a few had offered snippets, enough that they knew who Pearl was and they should avoid some bloke called Eddie. No photos had been provided, though, hence why Shawnee hadn't recognised the pair when they'd turned up. Now, she wished she'd asked Scott to send her one.

It was supposed to be a simple meeting for Scott to show Jet there was no funny business going on. He had drugs to sell, she wanted to buy them. But was Jet being so adamant about having a face-to-face meeting because she'd already suspected Andre wouldn't be the man who turned up? Shawnee and Scott had purposely stayed indoors as much as possible during the interactions he'd had on the phone with her — they were well aware that they could be being watched. Scott had gone out a couple of times in the car to drive around the block in the Audi, but he'd made sure to put sunglasses on because his eyes were the only thing that gave him away as not being Andre.

Shawnee could only speculate as to what had gone on, but she had bigger issues to worry about now that Jet and Pearl had come to her house in disguise and were still sitting out there, staring through the windscreen, their lips not moving.

They hadn't drunk the coffee. They'd worn gloves. Shawnee wasn't stupid—those women hadn't wanted to leave anything of themselves behind if they could help it. Why? Had they discovered what was really going on? She was told she wouldn't be seeing Scott again—was he banished or dead? And what did that mean for her? Would she be next?

How had they even found out she was involved in this? She'd taken nothing to Andre's house that would point to her identification. Had Scott been tortured last night and he'd blabbed? Why had they pretended to be Andre's cousins, though? Was it to see if she knew what was going on? She'd said she was Andre's cleaner—could they prove otherwise? And thank God she'd had the foresight to change her voice when she'd phoned Jet just now—the leader could now think Andre had some posh totty.

Unless the pair of them had been under surveillance for some time and Shawnee had been seen leaving Andre's house without her cleaning supplies. That hadn't happened often, so she'd be extremely unlucky if on the days she'd nipped home someone had been watching. She racked her brain to try and work out, if she hadn't been seen by any of Jet's people, how the fuck the woman had worked out she was in on things with Scott.

Martin.

Was that it? Had someone just happened to be watching the house when he'd come to collect the protection money and they'd followed his car and then stopped him to ask if he knew what her name was? The mention of paying leaders money…was that a warning that Shawnee was going to have to explain to the twins why she hadn't let them know she was running a cleaning business?

Why would Jet even do her a favour like that?

At last, Vittoria drove away, a small van popping into the slot as soon as she'd vacated it. That wasn't unusual, parking spaces were like gold dust around here. The signage on the side of the van was for a cleaning company, which gave

Shawnee the fucking creeps. Jet and Pearl had been in her house, and now a cleaning crew had turned up.

Was she about to be murdered and someone needed to clean up the blood?

The men walked up her garden path.

Her bell ding-donged.

Should she open up or run out the back?

Chapter Twelve

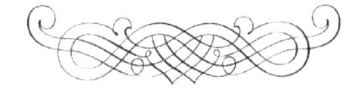

George was sure someone stood by the window in Shawnee's house, watching. A smudge of movement flitted between several of the blind slats, and he assumed she was coming to speak to them. Her dark shape appeared behind the panes of patterned glass in the front door, then moved away towards a square of light he guessed was a window at the end of the hallway, perhaps in the kitchen.

They'd made a mistake in not preparing better.

"She's going to do a runner. Stay there."

George darted down the street, dipping along an alley, high wooden fences either side. He came out into another alley that ran along the bottom of the rear gardens, looking left and right. Was he too late to catch her? A flash of colour to the right, then it disappeared around a left-hand corner. He gave chase, emerging onto a road that formed the top of a T with Shawnee's street. A double-decker bus pulled off, and with no sign of anyone around, he could only imagine she was on it.

"Fuck it."

He retreated to the alley but peered around to the street again to see whether she'd just hidden in the bushes in someone's garden and would come out because she thought he'd gone.

No one there except for an old lady whose white-haired head popped up above some scraggly hedges. "Oi," she called. "What are you doing over there?"

He didn't want to be noticed, but he had been, so now he was going to have to deal with it. "Did you just see a young black girl running along here by any chance?"

"What, on my hands and knees behind this fucking hedge? Not likely."

"No need to get bolshy. It was *you* asking *me* what I was doing. You're answering as if I'm bothering you. I didn't want to have a conversation with a snarky old cow, but you started it."

"Snarky old cow? You cheeky little bastard…"

He retreated farther into the alley so she couldn't see him, took his phone out, and quickly tapped a message to Will who he'd sent to keep watch outside Shawnee's house earlier. He told him to drive round here and park to wait and see if she appeared. A blue Fiat arrived at the junction, and once it drove past and George had seen Will inside, he ran back down the two alleys to meet with Greg.

"I think she got on the bus, but Will's round there keeping watch. I'll message for someone else to come here and sit in this street." He got on with that while he walked up the garden path.

Greg was already using the lock pick. By the time George had finished sending the message, his brother had gone inside. George followed, closing the door with his foot, then going upstairs to have a good scout around. It was a two-bed place, a nice tidy bathroom, the smallest bedroom an office. A laptop lay open on a desk underneath the window, and it had a separate keyboard and mouse that she'd plugged into the side. He wiggled the mouse, and the screen came to life with a Word document. He read the typed list.

If S hasn't made contact by lunchtime, go to house.
Collect the gear.
Leave body there?
Clean the house.

Maybe that's where she'd gone then, to Andre's.

George quickly sent a message to alert Moody, who currently sat outside Andre's, to keep an eye out for Shawnee. They'd sourced a picture of her from her Facebook page so everyone knew who to look out for.

Had she been making this list before Jet and Pearl had arrived? George and Greg had yet to ask the other leader what had been said here, but he'd told her on the phone they'd pick Shawnee up and take her back to their warehouse. Jet would meet them there.

He sent her an update.

GG: We've been held up. Shawnee legged it out the back. Intel found here suggests she's possibly gone to Andre's. Our man is looking out for her there. We're in her house.

Proust: Fucking hell! She almost had me believing she was just a cleaner! I'm wondering now whether that was her on the phone to me.

GG: What?

Proust: Someone claiming to be Andre's girlfriend rang me after we'd left Shawnee's. Didn't sound the same as her, though.

GG: Right, so an actual GF could be in the mix. fucking great. We'll continue to look through the house for more evidence but don't plan on being too long. We're mainly after drugs or money. If you need to be elsewhere for a while instead of hanging around at the warehouse, I'll let you know when we've arrived there and you can come back to try and identify the body with us.

Proust: We'll wait as we're already there.

George put his phone in his pocket and minimised the Word document, only to find another one underneath, but this wasn't a list. It contained seventy-two pages, and at the top of the one currently on the screen was today's date but nothing else written. He slowly scrolled back to page one, noting she didn't write something every day.

Friday February 23rd 2024

It's been three months today that I've been working for this prick. He's a fucking drug dealer! A. DRUG. DEALER! I know I've said it before in a previous entry, but fucking hell, it bears repeating because I've landed on my feet here. I think I've just about worked out how he operates, who comes to pick up and drop off and when, and I know all the PIN codes for everything I need to move forward.

I'm going to take over this man's life!

Now all I have to do is get Scott to agree to come in on this with me. Or, more to the point, teach him how to be more refined (and Italian LOL). His hair needs a trim to match Andre's, and he needs to grow stubble and get a fake tan, but in the right light he could seriously pass for Andre, especially if he has sunglasses on. Will Scott be able to pull it off, though? I could do it without him but only short-term. Eventually, someone will want to see Andre in the flesh, even if it's just on the phone.

I suppose I could say he's gone away and that's why I'm the one at the door taking the deliveries and handing the gear out. Surely, if I only need to use Scott for his voice when dealing with the current clients…there must be some software out there that would change mine to a man's? But that's not going to work for everything else. I need someone to think they've seen Andre every now and again. If he disappears completely, people are going to ask questions.

I'll ask Scott and see what he says. I'm sure once he knows how much money we can make out of this he can find it in his heart to pretend to be Italian. LOL!

I'm going to be rich, baby! Watch this space.

Was this a set of letters to someone? The use of *baby* pointed to the fact that it was, but maybe this was a diary entry instead and the word was only a figure of speech. Either way, it was obvious, now George was scrolling through the rest of the pages, that she'd documented how she'd pulled this scam off. He kept the laptop open in case closing it meant he'd need a password to get back in, then, to be on the safe side, decided to take pictures of all the pages so if something went wrong he'd at least have those. They'd make interesting reading.

He carried the still-open laptop downstairs to find Greg in the living room looking through a sideboard drawer. He found a small folder and opened it. Inside, a birth certificate and passport, both belonging to Shawnee. He put them back and shut the drawer.

"Got anything other than that?" George asked.

"Nope. You?"

"She kept either a diary or wrote emails in a Word doc before she sent them to whoever."

"And?"

"All this was her idea, she roped Scott into it."

"I wonder why he insisted on saying he was Andre then, even after he got caught? Is Shawnee some kind of nutter he was afraid of? Has she got other people in on this, men she uses to do the bully work, and he was scared of them? Honestly, I knew he was a sandwich short, but I would have thought he'd have blamed it on her if it was her brainchild in the first place, especially when he twigged he was going to die."

"Maybe he didn't believe Jet would really kill him. Whatever, he's dead now and is the least of our concerns. We've got a body to take out of a punchbag and Shawnee to round up and speak to. Oh, and I forgot to say she's probably going back to Andre's. There's a list on this laptop of things to do, and one of them is getting rid of a body."

Greg laughed. "She'll have a bloody hard job because it isn't there."

"The other is collecting the gear."

"Gear?" Greg frowned. "But we checked the house. Unless you and Pearl didn't bother looking in any cupboards."

"I admit we didn't in the snug, but I did in the kitchen and the units in the cellar. There was just the usual stuff in there. Did you check the loft?"

"No. Did you check inside cereal boxes and whatnot?"

"No… I was after a body not Coco Pops."

"Back to Andre's for a proper look then?"

George nodded. He'd read some more diary entries on the way.

Monday 15th July 2024

It's all very well knowing you need to kill someone, but when you've never done it before, it's pretty fucking scary even just planning it. I've got to get Scott in the house so he can hide and wait for Andre to come back, because let me tell you, I'm not doing this bit on my own, buddy. For a start, I'm not strong enough to defend myself if it goes wrong, and I also haven't got the strength to pick up a dead body and dispose of it.

This is where we're stuck. We don't know where to take it. There's all the different kinds of woods around here, but they have dog walkers, and someone's going to find him pretty quickly. Even if we bury him, a dog will most likely dig him up. We can't risk the body being found because that means my plan to slowly syphon Andre's money into an offshore account while still running his business and making even more cash would have to end.

The offshore account is something I've yet to look into. I wish I was some kind of mastermind who knew all this shit already, but you can't be blessed with everything, can you. I'm wondering if it means a trip on the dark web. Scott will know all about that, not to mention how I can get on there without anyone knowing I've done it.

So, back on track. A body means the police would be round his place like a shot, and they might even come to mine because I'm his cleaner and he's got my card on the fridge. Should I leave it there? I think so — neighbours will have seen me, and with all the video doorbells about, they'll eventually find me. I can get ruled out pretty quickly, although I might get asked questions regarding the amount of times I've been asked to open the front door lately, taking in the cardboard boxes that have been delivered but also passing out the smaller boxes to other people who come to collect them.

Could I be classed as an accessory? Surely not, if I make out I don't know what's in the boxes. There's no way I could say I haven't touched them because my fingerprints will be on them. Things will work out. It'll be all right.

So, the plan is to kill him and dispose of the body where he won't be found, or at least won't be found for a long time, and then once we hit a sticky spot where it looks like we're going to get caught for what we've done or people are being a little bit too nosy, we'll abandoned ship. We'll wait a few months after that, then I'll open another account for Scott and send him half the cash I'll have nicked.

I've got everything worked out apart from how Andre's going to die. It needs to be quick and clean. No blood. And it's going to happen on Friday 26th no matter what. I'm not prepared to keep putting this off.

"Looks like Andre died at the end of July last year," George said. "She said here on the fifteenth that it would be the twenty-sixth which was the following Friday."

"So that's been nine months since they bumped him off."

"The air in that punchbag smelled about right. Old death, know what I mean?"

<u>*Friday 26th July 2024*</u>

Scott didn't turn up. The stupid little prick bottled it, didn't he. I was going to do it on my own. I came up with the idea of whacking Andre on the back of the head with one of his hand weights in the gym. I know I said I didn't want any blood, but it's not like I can strangle him or something, is it. My arms would get too tired. Anyway, when I called Andre down to ask him if he wanted me to empty his storage cupboards down there and clean them out, I bottled it, too. I just couldn't do it.

I tried ringing Scott loads of times after I got home, and the fucking bastard wouldn't answer his phone, so I went down the Swan, and he was there at the bar drinking a pint as though nothing was wrong. I whispered to him and asked him what the fuck he was playing at, and he said he couldn't go through with it. We ended up going out the back for a ciggie, and I agreed I'd do the killing but he'd help me move the body. I don't expect him to become a murderer when it was my idea to do this in the first place, but I do expect him to earn some of the bloody money doing more than just walking around in a ponytail and sunglasses making out to Andre's neighbours that he's alive.

So we're going to have a proper chat tomorrow night and decide the method and the date it's going to happen.

"Did you find anything interesting?" Greg turned onto the estate where Andre lived.

"Not really, just that Scott chickened out of the actual killing, or should I say the night they first decided to do it, and she backed out, too."

"So what does that mean? That neither of them are hard-hearted? They were both scared? What?"

"I don't know, it basically says they couldn't go through with it, there wasn't an explanation why."

"Fucking frustrating."

"It would be even more frustrating if we didn't have these little insights into what was going on. She's basically confessing here; what more do you want? You being a grumpy bastard about this makes it seem like you're looking a gift horse in the mouth."

"I'm not!"

"You'd better not be."

"Or what?"

"I'll give you a Chinese burn." George smoothed his eyebrows. "The more I'm reading, the more I realise we should have known there was a different mastermind behind this than Scott. He just about had the brainpower to pretend to be Andre, but he definitely wasn't clever enough to have worked everything out the way Shawnee has. I kind of admire her to be honest. She's not shy in coming forward, I'll say that much for her."

George scanned the other entries until he found the one he was after.

<u>*Friday 16th August 2024*</u>

I did it. All by myself. I didn't use the hand weights in the end, and there was blood, but hey, I'm a cleaner, so it was okay.

We chose the 16th because Andre said he was staying in that night. He had a new customer coming to collect and wanted to at least be there for the first time. Plus it was three big cardboard boxes and he needed me to help him pick them up and hand them over because they were heavy. I *said to him I didn't even know if I would be there at eight when the bloke came to get the gear because I finish the cleaning by then, unless he wanted me to do something extra to pass the time. He said he could do with me removing the wine bottles downstairs and cleaning those and the racks and he'd give me an extra £70 for it plus throw in some dinner.*

This turned out really well. It meant I didn't have to sneak Scott in and hope Andre didn't catch us. Andre went out for kebabs as there's a shop only round the corner. I messaged Scott, and he came to the back door. I told him to go down in the cellar and wait at the end where the gym is. Andre came back, and we ate the kebabs, then I went down to start on the wine rack. The doorbell rang bit later on, which was the buyer, so we handed the boxes over. I went back down to the rack and waited for about twenty minutes and accidentally on purpose dropped a bottle of wine so I'd have to go upstairs to get the dustpan and brush.

Anyway, I explained what I'd done, and Andre went a bit pale when I told him which bottle I'd dropped. Apparently it was worth three grand, a few of them are, so that's another job for me because I'll be flogging them on eBay, ha-ha!

He started ranting and raving, throwing his arms up and shit like that, so I made out I was scared of him and ran to the gym. Scott had been hiding behind the wall of the archway, and as Andre came storming after me saying I owed him for the wine, Scott stuck his foot out and Andre tripped over it. He fell forward and smacked his temple on a pile of rectangular weights on his leg lift machine. It split his skin. There was blood.

Earlier on, while we'd been eating the kebabs, Scott had done what I asked and took the weights off the big dumbbells so there was just a long hollow pole. With Andre on the floor, I took the pole off Scott and whacked Andre on the head with it. He screamed and fell onto his back, putting a hand up to his temple and touching it and then looked to see all the blood on his fingers. I went over there with the pole and brought it end down on his face really hard. Some of it went into his head around his eye, on his cheek, and I had to yank it back out again. For some reason, Andre was snatching at his face like he wanted to grab the pain and throw it away, but instead he grabbed his eyeball. Jesus Christ, I've never seen something so gross in my life when he pulled it out.

I don't want to go into mega detail except that I ended up battering his head with the pole until he stopped breathing. I cleaned the pole after, then Scott put the weights back on it. I cleaned everything else. I got a towel and folded it up to put it under Andre's head so it caught any more blood. Then we were stuck with this body, not knowing where to put it, and I was thinking we'd have to keep him down there until he'd rotted or whatever, but it was going to stink. People who came to pick up the drugs might smell it.

Scott said about taking the stuffing out of the punchbag and putting Andre in it. He said if we wrapped him up tight in clingfilm so no more blood or whatever could come out, he might not smell then. I was willing to give it a go because it would save us taking the body out of the house. I was fucking knackered from killing him as it was, so carrying it at that point wasn't an option anyway.

So now he's wrapped up like a mummy and the punchbag is on the floor. I'll order a new one off Amazon because I quite enjoyed smacking the shit out of it whenever I went to work at the house.

The next phase can start on Monday. I'll go to the house as usual and deal with the customers. Scott can answer Andre's phone if it rings. I'll tell him to bring a toothbrush and shit with him because he may as well live there while I'm syphoning off the money week by week and making sure the drug business ticks over smoothly.

I just want enough to buy myself a fuck-off house and then I'm out of there. Who knows, by then, Andre might be bones.

"She sounds like an utter psycho," George said.

Greg parked a couple of doors down from Andre's house. "Why?"

"She's only gone and detailed what she did. From what I can gather, she could have gone into even more gory detail, as in the murder was worse than what she wrote, but what she put was enough."

"Which was?"

"She battered Andre to death with a pole from some fucking dumbbells."

Greg barked out a laugh. "At least she's original."

"And he pulled his own eyeball out."

"You're talking about this as if you've never had anything to do with something like that before."

"It's a bit shocking when you read about someone else doing it. When you do it yourself it's not so bad."

"It's bad whoever does it."

"And it's especially bad because she was doing it to steal Andre's money. I mean, fair play to the girl, she certainly knows how to work an angle, but fuck me sideways, if we weren't going after her to kill her for what she's done—and she *needs* to be killed—then we could use her in our own business."

George put the pieces together and went on to explain how she must have made a fortune.

"I want the details of that offshore account—if she even ended up opening one," Greg said.

"Are we going to nick the dosh?"

"Too fucking right. Andre owes us protection money. So does she."

"You'd better hope Shawnee and Scott haven't spent it all."

"Maybe the deal with Jet was because they were running out of cash," Greg suggested.

"No, it says here she wanted enough to buy a house, so she'll have been saving." George got out of the van and popped the laptop in the back, closing the lid now he'd read what he'd needed to. He had enough verbal ammunition to throw at Shawnee when they caught up with her.

They quickly hustled inside the house.

"Did you see Moody out there?" Greg asked. "He's taken a leaf out of our book and gone with a beard and a wig today."

George walked into the living room and looked out of the window. Moody sat in a gold Hyundai apparently reading a newspaper. Greg came over and peered out himself. George watched the street for any signs that someone hid and, seeing nothing, checked their work phone to see if Moody had sent any messages. While he was at it, he sent one to Jet.

GG: You might want to go home.

Proust: How come?

GG: We're at Andre's. More shit has come to light, so we might be here for a while. Or you can come over and help us look for any gear plus information regarding Andre's bank account. Shawnee's been paying herself from it, possibly into an offshore account. I want to know what that account number is.

Proust: We'll come to you. More hands make light work or however the saying goes.

GG: Many hands.

Proust: Whatever.

Chapter Thirteen

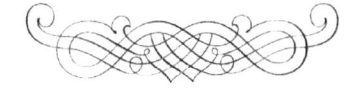

Ward F buzzed with curiosity regarding the new person who'd come in. Miranda had seen people arriving so often now that she'd like to say it failed to pique her interest, but that would be a big fat lie. Fuck all went on around here, so when it did, almost everyone was eager to join in. Most people, even some of the proper nutters on floor three, had

come down to level one and sat in the reception area or stood leaning against the walls. Nurse Nora had already swept by to tell them to return to their rooms, but she was never really one to completely enforce the rules, so the patients ignored her.

Patients? More like inmates.

Two orderlies stood either side of the woman who'd been brought in from the main hospital, the doors clunking as they locked behind them. She appeared spaced out, her brown hair wild as though she'd previously been in a bit of a state and no one had helped to tidy her up. It was matted and stuck up in all directions, and one side of her face had a cut going from the inside of her eye to her jawline by her ear. Visible stitches made it look worse than it probably was. Thin to the point of emaciation, her wrist bones sticking out, her hospital nightie and dressing gown drawing even more attention to her haphazard state, the poor cow didn't have much going for her. Miranda was tempted to step forward and offer to be her 'ward buddy' but needed to know exactly what she'd be dealing with first. She could be heading to level three; she could be a complete nutter.

"Right, everyone," Nora said, "this is Catalina, and she'll be on level two. She doesn't need a buddy just

yet, she needs sleep and some time to settle in, so one will be selected tomorrow."

The orderlies led a shuffling Catalina to the lift, using a special code to open the doors, Nurse Nora getting on there with them. The doors closed, and about thirty patients milled around, clearly deflated there had been no excitement, no Catalina kicking off, screaming that she didn't want to be sectioned. Maybe that had happened before she'd been brought here, hence her drugged-up state.

Nurse Bert, a forty-something, watched the proceedings from his spot behind the reception desk, a couple of orderlies with him ready to jump in should anyone have a mind to start trouble. No one seemed inclined to do so, most of them biding time until their release and not wanting to rock the boat, many having conversations and acting like they weren't standing in the reception of a mental ward but in a pub.

Miranda would never get over how this place worked. It was a community all by itself, with its own laws, and it was surprising how quickly she'd got used to the routine. Even though she didn't want to be here, it had been a safe place for her to grieve, if that's what she'd even been doing. She wasn't sure because she doubted grieving meant being happy that your mother was dead. Normal people didn't feel that way, but then she never professed she was normal. She reckoned she'd been different since the day she'd been born.

So she didn't go down a dangerous mental path, she glanced around for Alicia, but she must have decided to stay on level two and forgo watching any dramatic entertainment the new patient may have brought. She enjoyed reading and keeping to herself a lot, especially since Thompson's announcement that she was assessing everyone to get to know them. All Alicia wanted to do now was behave herself, keep her head down, and then be set free once her medication had proved to be the correct type. For the whole time Alicia had been here, she'd been detained so that they could monitor her reaction to the tablets she'd been given. They'd wanted to only send her home once they knew she could live as near perfect life as she could had she not been bipolar.

Val had left a couple of weeks ago; Thompson hadn't stood in her way after all. Miranda reckoned Alicia missed the older woman more than she let on. They'd bonded pretty well, Alicia perhaps seeing Val as a mother figure. They planned to meet up once Alicia was out. They'd asked Miranda to join them, but she had a feeling that when the punters knew she'd returned home she'd be busier than ever, so she'd been vague about making concrete plans.

Funny how she'd been desperate for friends and then when she had them she would most likely cast them aside in order to make money instead. In reality, all she wanted to do was stay in the house as much as possible, entertain the men, and keep herself away from anyone who could section her again. So long as she kept clean from drugs and drink, everything would be okay.

She'd be leaving this time next week. Thankfully, Thompson agreed with Charlene's assessment. The social worker had contacted the council to let them know Miranda would be returning home, so there was no need to reassess her housing situation. She'd also popped in to see Bunty who'd promised to make sure there were some essential shopping items ready for when Miranda arrived. It had all been a bit exciting at first, until Thompson had flexed her claws, showing everyone she couldn't be trusted because she'd rescinded her promise to someone else, refusing him release the day before he was due to leave. Miranda would be on tenterhooks until she was actually on the bus moving farther and farther away from here.

She wandered over to take one of the spare seats as a few patients had moved into the common room on level one. Baldy Ben, a chubby man with wobbly jowls, spotted her and smiled. His shiny royal-blue, flare-

legged jumpsuit was too tight in the nether region, the seam digging in. He swooped in and sat beside her, his forearms across his knees, his head jutting forward on his thick neck. She should have been paying more attention as to who was around her when she'd sat. If she'd seen him then she wouldn't have gone anywhere near him. He lived on level three and wasn't as crazy as the majority of the others but definitely loopier than Miranda who'd now been moved to level one.

He'd told her last week that he believed he was the president of a country she'd never heard of, and that with him being 'incarcerated', as he put it, his spies would infiltrate England and find him, taking him back to his palace. She told him that kings had palaces, and he'd shot her down by saying if he wanted to have a palace then he could bloody well have one, no matter what she said.

"They'll be here later," he said as if they'd already been talking about it prior to her sitting down.

"What time?" She'd found it was pointless telling him he wasn't a president and there were no spies. A lot of the people from level three believed certain things, and to try to convince them otherwise could do more harm than good, according to Nora. A bit like with dementia patients, it was better to live with them in their reality.

"Four o'clock," he whispered. "My vice president contacted me…" He leaned even closer. "Via the secret wire."

Ah, the secret wire was back in play again. She resisted rolling her eyes; it wasn't his fault he believed these things. Everyone knew an orange was orange, and that was how he viewed the things he believed in. To him, they were true—the secret wire actually existed.

"I see." She smiled at him. "Good job you remembered to charge it then, otherwise he wouldn't have been able to speak to you and let you know."

Baldy shook his head and tutted. "It's self-charging. It takes energy from the air around it. You don't even need to plug it in anywhere."

"I wasn't aware of that."

"Yes you were. I told you last time we talked, which was Wednesday at two-thirteen p.m. at the reception desk."

"You didn't tell me, but not to worry."

He stood and plonked his hands on his hips, staring down at her. "Lying to the president is treason."

Miranda was about to argue that she wasn't lying but remembered how Baldy could get a bee in his bonnet about some things. She didn't have the energy to argue the toss with him. Instead, she said goodbye and wandered towards the stairs that were set inside a glass-walled rectangular area in the centre of the building so patients could be seen going up and down them at all times. They weren't allowed to use the lift unless they were with a doctor, nurse, or orderly.

She went to level two where she found Alicia sitting on an armchair by the window—the window that wasn't facing the hospital building. The view was breathtaking here, even though blocks of flats and skyscrapers filled the distant horizon. Here were the grounds, all greenery and trees, although from the windows facing the front of the building it was car after car in the parking area.

Miranda sat and watched two people sitting on a bench beside a fish pond, smoking. They were likely visitors waiting to come in for two o'clock. She hadn't seen them before, so maybe they were here for Catalina.

"Before you fill me in, I saw who came," Alicia said. "Nora brought her over to me before she was taken to her room. She asked me to be her ward buddy, so that means I'm stuck here for at least a fortnight."

"Ah, mate, I'm really sorry to hear that. Think about it, though, you've done really well to be chosen as a buddy at last. That means you're considered almost normal."

"Lucky me."

They both laughed and continued to stare out of the window.

"What will you do when you're out?" Alicia asked.

"What else can I do but get hold of the punters and see if they want to come back? I don't know how to do anything else."

Alicia sighed. "I can't imagine going back to work. I feel like I've been institutionalised already."

"You could work from home."

"I suppose."

They lapsed into silence.

Miranda broke it with: "Baldy said his spies are coming here later to break him out."

Alicia snorted. "They can break me out at the same time. I'll go and live in his palace with him."

"It's fucking stupid that us two are here. We're not even mad."

"I acted it until I got on the tablets."

"True, but you know what I meant. You're not insane-insane.*"*

"Maybe Baldy isn't really. Maybe he just needs the right meds, too."

It was a nice thought, that. But Miranda had seen one too many times that medication didn't solve everything. Some people were madder than a box of frogs regardless, trapped in whatever reality their brain had created for them. She admired all the employees who worked here trying to make their lives better, but fucking hell, she couldn't wait to get out.

A commotion at the door drew her attention. Baldy came thundering across the common room with his fingers and thumb cocked as if he held a gun. He stood in front of them and jerked his head. "Get up, nice and slow, no funny moves."

Nora hovered by the door where she must have followed him. Miranda sighed and did as she was told.

"And you," he said to Alicia.

"I'm not in the mood to play your games, Ben." Alicia seemed so tired, the bone-weary type of knackered where she wanted to sleep all of her problems away.

"But it's lunchtime," Baldy said, his tone changing from important president to a young lad, "and if you don't get down there quick you'll miss out on the jelly. It's jelly day, you remembered that, didn't you?"

Alicia let out a long breath and stood. The jelly had swung it, she loved it, but her face hadn't yet got the memo. She didn't crack a smile, instead walking along beside Baldy who'd gone back into president mode and pressed the tips of his fingers against her arm to let her know he was about to shoot her if she didn't allow him to lead her down the stairs. Miranda trailed behind with Nora, thanking her lucky stars she was getting out of here in a matter of days.

If she stayed any longer, she might actually go mad.

Chapter Fourteen

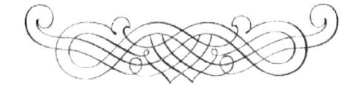

Shawnee was still shitting herself. She'd got on a bus across Cardigan to Andre's and then walked down his street. A man had stared at her from a bronze-coloured car, so she'd put her head down and kept going. She should have realised Jet would've put someone outside to keep watch. The man hadn't seemed to recognise her, though, but that could be because she'd found her work turban in her pocket, the one she used to keep dust off her hair when she cleaned. She'd put it on along with her glasses, which always changed her appearance enough that some people didn't recognise her, especially without her Afro on show. She'd made her way around the back, hoping to get in that way, and just as she'd slid a key into the lock of the bifold doors, she'd heard the front door closing with its distinctive echoing snap. She'd quickly retreated, hopped on another bus, and now stood two streets away outside a Spar, shaking and wondering what to do next.

She had to calm down and think straight.

One: those men from the cleaning van would have gone through her house by now, realised she wasn't there, and may well have nicked some of her stuff.

Two: The man in the bronze car was probably something to do with Jet and would be watching Andre's house for God knew how long.

Three: It was just as well she hadn't gone inside Andre's because someone would have found her there eventually—well, someone had definitely got in via the front and were likely there to wait for her.

Unless it was Scott.

She remembered leaving her laptop open to go and answer the door when the so-called Vittoria and Aurora had come calling. Fuck it, she didn't have a passcode or PIN for the bloody thing, so if they woke the screen up they'd know what she'd been working on. They'd see her diary entries, something she'd planned to destroy once this was all over. If the cleaning blokes were Jet's men then they were likely to tell her, or show her, what she'd written when they caught up with her, so there was no way she could worm out of it and say it was all Scott's idea.

Why had she been so bloody stupid in needing to write it all down? It was more an obsession because she'd read it over and over again, seeing where she went wrong and where she could have done better.

Where could she go now to lie low for a bit? It wasn't like she was destitute. She had the money in the offshore account, and she had a couple of thousand in her own. The house in Foxton Avenue had come to her via her mum who'd died. It had a legacy tenancy with the council so she was able to take it over. She wasn't overly attached to the stuff inside, it was all cheap and cheerful furniture from Argos or IKEA, but she wouldn't mind having her passport and birth certificate which were in the drawer in the living room sideboard.

Providing those men had gone, could she get in and out without being seen, or, like at Andre's, had Jet posted a man outside? Or *men*, front and rear? No one had been out the back when she'd run away earlier, and she hadn't spotted anyone sitting out the front either while she'd been on the phone to Jet, but that didn't mean they weren't there now.

Scott must have told Jet everything last night, and it wasn't a surprise, not really. He'd never wanted to be involved in Andre's murder. He hadn't minded impersonating him but wasn't keen on going to the art gallery. He'd felt they could just wipe out Andre's account at the point Jet had insisted on a meeting, and if Shawnee hadn't been so fucking greedy then they'd both be free and clear. Instead, she'd wanted whatever money Jet was happy to part with, and now look what had happened.

She was going to have to go to her nan's, but no, that was a risk because Jet knew exactly who Shawnee was, and it wouldn't be hard for a woman like her to find out the information she needed—family members, all that. Nan would pretend Shawnee wasn't there, Nan was a con artist herself, but it wasn't fair to put her in that position. So who else was there? She could sofa surf with a couple of friends, or there was that lad, Puggy, who stored and sold drugs for Andre. But there was that pair of balaclava bastards Andre paid to keep an eye on Puggy. What if they came round while she was there, nosing?

Puggy had some kind of chronic health issues, maybe mental ones, too. Would he keep it quiet if she offered him money to stay in his spare room? He had a ground-floor flat, which was handy for her if she needed to make a quick escape because he had a garden. She'd keep herself busy by cleaning the place, as last time she'd gone round there on the pretext she was delivering drugs for Andre, it had been a shithole.

In a day or two, she'd work out what to do next.

She wasn't exactly sure what Puggy had been diagnosed with, but he dribbled a lot, his bottom lip hung limp, and he came across a bit thick in the head. He took things literally and didn't understand sarcasm or jokes, so she'd probably find it difficult being in his company after a while. There was absolutely no reason for anyone to think she'd come here. Her dealings with Puggy had been minimal in the past; she'd dropped boxes here, then had a cup of tea, and that was that.

She'd taken a convoluted route, dipping down alleys and darting into side streets so if anyone was following her they'd hopefully got lost. She stuck her head down as she walked past the row of windows of the ground-floor flats in the high-rise block, hands in her pockets, her stride fast. He lived in number two, so she tapped on the door, nervous that he might be out. She was sure he'd mentioned some kind of physio he had to have in order to stop his muscles doing something or other.

The door opened, and he stared at her in his light-blue tracksuit bottoms and matching sweatshirt, blinking, clearly trying to work out why she was there when they hadn't agreed for her to make another delivery yet. But had her turban and glasses thrown him? Was he trying to work out who she was?

Honest to God, he looked so dumb and vacant, she was surprised he was allowed to live by himself—not only that, it was a wonder he was clever enough to even sell drugs. Then again, all he had to do was hand baggies out at the front door and take the money which he passed on to the two men Andre had employed.

Puggy was being used because of his situation. He was basically being exploited. Her still bringing drugs here or sending them to him by courier meant she was just as bad as Andre. She had strong views about people like Puggy being left to fend for themselves when it was so obvious they needed a carer. If she was a nicer person she'd offer to come and visit him every now and again to make sure he was okay, but she couldn't be bothered.

He got benefits, and she paid him well for selling the drugs. He had on a pair of Nike Air Jordans that cost over one hundred and fifty quid. Didn't the social worker or whatever wonder where he'd got them from? His clothes were Nike as well.

"Nobody told me you would be here," he said.

She pushed past him, nervous about being kept outside even though she was semi disguised. "Shut the bloody door, will you?"

She shouldn't bark at him like that, it wasn't his fault she was impatient and worried about being spotted. He did as he was told but kept glancing at the door as though he expected Andre to turn up any second—or the two men.

"Do Fish and Chips know you're here?" he asked.

A headache was going to start up soon if she wasn't careful. She had a bit of an aura going on. "What are you on about?"

"That's what they said their names are, Fish and Chips."

She leaned against the kitchen doorframe. "Are they the men who come here to make sure you're selling the drugs like a good boy for Andre?"

"Yeah. I'm not allowed to tell the social services, or the lady who comes round to make sure I've got my medicine, but they're not really called Fish and Chips. I've told everyone they're my friends."

A lady who comes round to make sure he's got his medicine. Fuck. "When does the medicine lady come round?"

"Every Wednesday morning at ten o'clock, or sometimes it's three minutes past, it depends on whether the traffic lights round the corner are on red, because if they are then it means she's got to stop. It's the law that she's got to stop."

Wednesday. That was okay, Shawnee didn't plan to be here by then.

"Do you think you could keep a secret?" she asked him.

His eyes lit up, and he fiddled with his fingers. "What kind of secret?"

"The kind where you don't tell anybody where I am."

"Why would I even tell anyone where you are? I don't know where you live and I don't even know your name. You're just the lady who brings the boxes, and if you don't bring them, then the man on the motorbike does."

"Can I trust you to know my name?" she asked.

He nodded. "Yeah."

"It's Shawnee, and I need to stay here for a bit, see, with you, which is why you can't tell anyone where I am."

"Are you hiding here?"

"For a little while."

"Have you done something bad, or does someone want to do something bad to you?"

"It doesn't matter, I just need you to keep me a secret for a while. I'll give you some money for having me here, and it'll be enough for us to have takeaways, and I'll clean the flat for you. The last time I came to drop off stuff for Andre, you were saying the lady from the social was worried you might not be able to live on your own anymore because of the mess. You were crying because you didn't want to go into a care place. Do you remember?"

"Yeah."

It wasn't as much of a tip now, so either he'd had a good go at tidying up himself or the social had sent someone round to help him, but it was a far cry from what it should be. It didn't smell very nice, as if he didn't open the windows, ever, and a glance through to the living room showed he seemed to think his dirty washing belonged on the floor. Three knee-height piles of Domino's pizza boxes were stacked beside the front door in a row underneath coats hanging from a rack of hooks. He was using the boxes as a piece of furniture, a large fruit bowl on top with keys in it, his electric and gas smart meter display unit beside it.

"I could get you something nice to go there so you don't have to have the pizza boxes, Puggy. What do you think? Shall we give this place a glow-up? I bet Fish and Chips will be impressed when they come round next. They'll think you're well glam."

Puggy smiled, displaying wonky teeth and large pale gums. He dribbled a bit and cuffed it away with his sweatshirt sleeve. "Fish and Chips can't know you're here."

"No, I'm not here."

"But you are."

"Yes, but we're *pretending* I'm not." *Fucking hell!*

"Who do I say did the glow-up then?"

"You did."

"But that's hard work and I don't want to."

"You don't have to, it'll be me."

"But you just said it'll be me."

Shawnee wanted to punch him. "I know, but *I'll* do the glow-up, *you* just have to pretend you did it because I'm not supposed to be here, am I? It's a secret because I need to hide from nasty people." *Shit, I didn't mean to say that last bit. Will he back out now?*

"Ahh, I get it." He frowned. "Will the nasty people come here and look for you?"

"Why would they do that? No one knows I'm here."

"Okay, that's all right then. I was just checking because Fish was mean to me last month, and I got a fat lip and a black eye."

"Oh dear."

"Where will you be if someone comes round?"

"I'll hide in your spare bedroom. In the built-in cupboard where you told me to put the cardboard boxes with the baggies in them."

"Okay."

"Right, you stick the kettle on, and I'll start cleaning the kitchen. While you're at it, think about what you want for dinner and maybe have a look on Argos for that unit in the hallway. They've probably got one for shoes. That'll be handy, won't it. If we can put them in there then it means you won't trip over your trainers that are all over the floor."

"Miss Daulton from the social will be happy."

I'll be happy, too, if you keep your gob shut.

Tonight, she'd nip home to collect her passport and birth certificate when it got dark. What she'd do after that was a thought for another day.

Chapter Fifteen

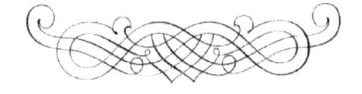

Pearl scratched her head from where the wig itched. She couldn't wait for this day to end so she could take it off, but like Jet had said earlier while they'd been waiting outside the warehouse, it was best they stay in disguise.

They'd been through Andre's house, gloves on, looking through absolutely every nook and cranny to try and find money or drugs. In one of this bedrooms on the top floor was a small office, a laptop George had easily accessed. He'd clicked every icon saved on the Google browser, checking where each one led—almost all of them were for bank websites, although no passwords had been saved to the device.

Now they were all down in the cellar. Pearl's job was to take out the wine bottles to see if anything had been hidden behind them in the racks. Jet and Greg were in the middle section taking everything out of the storage cupboards, and George was looking at the gym equipment. By the time Pearl had removed every wine bottle, her hands sweated beneath the latex gloves. She turned to look at the piles of toilet rolls and cans and things behind her, and it felt like they'd made a big mess for no reason. She continued her task, peering at all the empty spaces where the wine bottles had rested. Nothing but wall behind them. She sighed at the thought of putting all the bottles back, but George wanted the house left as they'd found it, so she had no choice.

He came to check their progress and frowned at a cupboard Greg had just emptied. George popped his head back round the archway into the gym, then back to study the cupboard.

"The wall on the gym side goes back farther than the back of the cupboards. Check if there's false panels."

Greg and Jet stepped forward, tapping away and trying to slide the wood across. George reached out and pressed the wood in another cupboard, and it sprang forward like a door. Pearl walked over there to see what was behind it.

Stack after stack of cocaine bricks in clingfilm, which explained why there'd been enough clingfilm in the house to wrap the body.

"That'll do nicely." George looked at Jet. "We'll split it between us."

"But it was found on your Estate," Jet said.

"But you were expecting to buy product and you couldn't, so here's the product. We're working together on this, so shut up and take what's on offer."

"Thank you."

Pearl jerked a thumb over her shoulder. "There's nothing behind the wine racks, so I'll put the bottles away."

George and Greg got on with popping the coke bricks in black bags. When they carried them out to the van in a bit, it would look like they were removing rubbish after cleaning. Once Jet had refilled the cupboards and Pearl had slid the last bottle away, they wandered upstairs to go out the front for some fresh air. They stood on the pavement, sunglasses lowered, Jet vaping and blowing out candy-floss-scented clouds.

"Are they always this nice?" Pearl asked quietly in case they came out with more bags and caught her talking about them. "The twins, I mean. Sharing the…packages…not many people would do that."

"There's a misconception about those two, but they don't necessarily want it to be common knowledge—they're bastards with hearts. If you're on their good side, then you'll be okay, but if you're not…"

"I can imagine. Part of me keeps wanting to tell the other girls from the house who rescued us. I'm not going to, obviously, but I feel so much better knowing it was them rather than some random red disciple who had a bone to pick with the High Priest. For some reason the idea of that was really creepy, but knowing it's the twins isn't creepy at all."

She shuddered at the memory of those people dressed in cloaks with white masks on their faces. They'd all paid a lot of money to join in on rituals, women laid out stone slabs in the middle of nowhere, the customers using them for sexual gratification. The High Priest hadn't been anyone to fear in the end, just some young kid playing at being a big man, but during the time she'd lived at the house he'd ruled their lives and had been very much feared.

Jet nodded. "I can understand that, but I promise you, their involvement needs to stay a secret because they'll have likely killed people or at least hurt them in order to find you. With there being an undercover copper involved, it stands to reason why you can't say anything. Why should the twins go to prison when they did a good thing? And they would, because I doubt very much that copper would keep her mouth shut if you told her the Cardigan leaders had marched in with army clothes on and holding those fucking big guns. For a start she'd want to know where the guns had come from, and that will be a can of worms you don't want to open."

Pearl nudged Jet to stop her from saying anything else. A blonde woman tottered down the street on skyscraper-high heels carrying a beige Pomeranian that looked like it had just been to the doggy hairdresser's. Its owner stared Pearl and Jet up and down, overtly assessing them. She walked past, then stopped a couple of paces away, turning to face them.

"Is everything all right?" she asked in a posh accent.

In other words, what the fuck are you doing in my street?

"Yes, why would it not be?" Jet said, Italian Vittoria back in full force. She flicked at one side of her wig so the hair rested on her back.

"It's just that we don't usually have people standing in the street smoking those ghastly things. We're a better class than that."

Jet stiffened as though she wanted to punch the woman's head in and struggled to hold back the urge. "I was not aware I was not allowed to smoke on the street. Our cousin told me it would be okay, otherwise I would not be doing it."

Perfectly arched eyebrows lifted, then they lowered slightly into a frown—or what could be classed as a frown when someone's forehead had been Botoxed to death. "Your cousin?"

"Yes, Andre, the man who lives just there."

"Oh, him. A charming man. Always says hello if he sees me. He did so last night, actually, when he was on his way out." She turned to inspect the row of cars. "I don't see his Audi here…"

"He has gone to Italy for a holiday. He is staying in our house while we oversee the cleaning done in his."

The woman looked at the twins' van. "That's not the company he usually uses. There's a woman called Shawnee who comes."

"She has not got time to fit in a deep clean, plus Andre is donating a lot of his clothing to charity, they are now out of season, so we have been putting it in black bags."

This seemed to satisfy her. "I see. Well, I'd better be off."

Blondie walked away and entered a house three doors down, giving them a sly glance just as she shut the door. Pearl sighed in relief—she knew Jet well enough to know she'd wanted to kick off spectacularly, tell her to mind her own fucking business. She was so used to not being questioned on her own Estate that putting up with it on someone else's was obviously difficult.

"We need to get the fuck out of here before I lose my shit," Jet muttered.

The twins appeared with black bags; they must have been waiting for Blondie to bugger off, but now she'd probably be at her window, watching.

"Be as quick as you can," Jet told them as they went past. "Nosy neighbour alert. If anyone around here asks you questions, we're revamping Andre's wardrobe and those black bags are full of clothes."

Jet led the way inside, cursing about them having latex gloves on again like they had at Shawnee's, but at least here Blondie may have thought they were wearing them because they were helping with the cleaning, which was a bit of a joke considering they were dressed up to the nines. But what did it matter? They were in disguise, and it wasn't like they'd be back here after all the drugs had been removed, was it. The woman and the dog could go and fuck themselves as far as Pearl was concerned.

In the cellar of the twins' warehouse, which had a completely different vibe compared to the one at Andre's (the walls dripped with condensation for a start), Pearl listened to George talking on the phone. He was arranging for someone to get a few men together and go in search of Shawnee, telling them to ask questions in the hope that the location where she was hiding would be revealed.

"Start with family. Mason let us know earlier that her nan lives in Cobden Road. Someone go and relieve Moody—I want him going to the nan's. I'll send him a message to let him know what's what. Otherwise, it's the usual scouting around until we've sniffed the little bitch out."

He ended the call and sliced through the clingfilm in the punchbag. Jet covered her nose with both hands, so Pearl did the same. George only cut enough to reveal a face, but there was no way to identify the person because the features were in such a state.

"I had a feeling we weren't going to get very far on this," George said. "In her diary or whatever the fuck it was, Shawnee said she'd beaten him with a dumbbell pole, and it looks to me like she basically obliterated his face. I should imagine any of his identification and his phone and whatnot have probably been used by Scott, so I don't think we're going to find anything on the body that can prove it's Andre. We're just going to have to take it as a given."

"Check the whole of the remains anyway, then cut it up and put it in the Thames," Greg said. "I'll fire up the wood burner for the clingfilm and the bag."

Pearl went upstairs while that went on—the smell wasn't particularly strong but it was revolting, sticking in the back of her throat. She sat at a long table and passed the time by counting the boxes halfway up the wall on a balcony that went round.

Jet joined her a few minutes later. "There's a wallet in his pocket with a medical exemption card in it, Andre's name on the front. What did he have wrong with him where he was allowed free prescriptions? Not that it matters now, he's bloody dead. Let's go and split that coke and get it taken home." She held up the twins' van keys. "I've agreed with George and Greg that we'll come back once they've found Shawnee, although I'm going to get my men on it as well, like I said. Now we've got the gear, we can meet our buyers tomorrow after we've checked it for quality and our lads have re-bagged it all, but I'll drop you off so you can have some rest. It's been a mental day, and you can bet she'll be found by dark, so we need a breather in the meantime. If she's not, I'll be highly surprised."

Pearl nodded, glad to be going home.

Who knew being a gangster was such hard work.

Chapter Sixteen

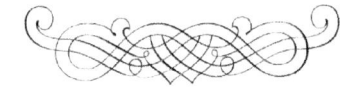

It was pretty shocking that life in Ward F had been forgotten so quickly. Miranda did think about Alicia, Val, and everyone else from time to time, but her stay there had become a distant memory faster than she'd imagined it would. When she'd lived there she'd thought she'd never forget it, the routine, the tears, the frustration of being stuck somewhere she didn't want

to be, where she didn't even think she should be. She'd learned that when you were in the midst of a situation it consumed you, but once you were no longer in it, you could easily pretend it hadn't happened.

Life at home had been busy enough that she concentrated on that and not much else. The majority of customers had returned, happy enough to use the back alley and tap on the kitchen door rather than go around the front. She'd explained that she'd been informed a nosy neighbour was likely to grass her up for running a knocking shop, and they'd accepted her explanation without a quibble. Of course they bloody had. None of them wanted to be caught with their pants down by the police.

She'd slept with men one hundred and three times since her release—maybe she'd taken to counting them as a leftover from Ward F where she'd marked down the days towards the six-month point when she was more likely to be released. Or maybe keeping a tally of the men had come from something Alicia had whispered to her when they'd said their goodbyes on level two.

"Give yourself one thousand times, save as much of the money as you can, then get out of the trade."

It wasn't a bad idea. If she charged them one hundred quid a visit, no caving on that price, no cheapies, she'd earn one hundred thousand, and when she broke it down like that, it was a staggering amount of money. Yes, she'd have household expenses, but her benefits would pay for those. If she saved enough she could pay for a university course.

She could be someone who wasn't ashamed of what she did for a living.

She told herself off for that thought. She should never *be ashamed, she should be proud of who she was no matter what, but she'd seen the way the neighbours had looked at her when she'd arrived home from Ward F, scorn on their faces as though they were just waiting for her to start opening her legs to all and sundry again. Bunty had been round a few times, mainly to drop by teabags, milk, or a loaf of bread which Miranda paid her for. She'd never be like her mother in that way. She'd always pay.*

Miranda had explained her reasoning to Bunty who understood—or she'd said she did anyway—that getting a few quid under her belt was the way to go before moving forward to a better life. The problem was, Miranda had developed a shopping addiction now, one she indulged in on a Saturday morning, going into town and walking into high-end shops, buying designer handbags, clothes, and shoes. Stupid of her when barely anyone ever saw her in them, but they made her feel good about herself.

Then Bunty had come round with yet another warning. "Her over the road has been watching, seeing you coming back in a taxi with them posh carrier bags. If you're going to go shopping in places like that then take other bags with you to put your stuff in, like the ones from Aldi or whatever."

Miranda had poured her a cup of tea and passed it over. "Thanks for the heads-up—again. It's come at the right time actually, because the spending is getting out of control, it means I'm not saving like I should be."

"It's understandable that you'd want to splurge to begin with," Bunty had said, "considering your mum didn't exactly dress you very nice as you were growing up and you tended to go without, but that's it now, okay? You've got a life plan, you know where you want to be, and while you're making easy money at the moment, I really do worry about what it's doing to your mental health—what you're doing to earn that money."

Miranda had opened her mouth to argue about that, but Bunty had held her hand up to stop her.

"Hear me out. You were going to bite my head off before you heard what I was actually going to say,

weren't you. I don't mean your mental health in that you'd need to go back to that bloody hospital, I meant your well-being and how you feel about yourself."

Miranda tucked that altercation away in her mind and finished getting ready for this evening's work. It was an eight-hundred-pound night, that amount of cash was nothing to be sniffed at, and she'd bought a cheap safe to pop all her cash in, putting it on a shelf in the larder in the kitchen behind the Coco Pops, somewhere none of the punters would see it. She'd revamped Mum's room, using it for work, and it had helped her head space a lot, having a different bed to sleep in to the one she shared with the men.

While she had some time before the first customer arrived, she used her new laptop to look up news stories about Mr Swanson and what he'd done to her mother. Bunty said she shouldn't torment herself, but what the next-door neighbour didn't know was that Miranda was trying to feel *something normal people would, anything, but sadly, all she experienced was a hot internal rage directed towards a mother who, had she done something different for a living, would never have been killed. Sometimes, Miranda wondered whether that day so many years ago when Mum had laughed at his gift of flowers had been the start of her downfall.*

Had he harboured a grudge ever since? Had she regularly laughed at him whenever he'd visited? Had she emasculated him? Had she made him feel that she was superior to him, even though it was the other way around? Mr Swanson was well-to-do, well-spoken, and Mum was, quite frankly, from the wrong side of the tracks compared to him.

Something else had come out that Miranda hadn't heard about until she'd read one of the articles. Mr Swanson had been waiting outside in his car and had seen Miranda leaving the house to go to the shop. He'd also seen the customer leave, and he knew, because he apparently spied on the house a lot, that Miranda wouldn't be out for long and he only had a limited amount of time before she came back. In his first interview he'd said he wanted Mum to let him look after her, so they could be a couple, but in this *article it stated he'd gone there with the intention of killing her.*

If he couldn't have her, no one could.

She sat with her feelings for a moment and once again felt no empathy towards the woman who had given birth to her. Maybe Bunty was right and it would take time—and probably maturity—for Miranda to find some sympathy somewhere, but that day wasn't today. She had men to service and money to earn, and trying to mourn her mother just wasn't on the cards.

Showered and in fresh-smelling pyjamas, cosy and warm, Miranda lay in her bedroom in the dark, staring at a ceiling she couldn't see. Sleep was being an elusive bastard, swooping in to take her away but then her mind perked up with some insignificant fact that she pondered, chasing the sandman off.

This particular fact had really brought on unease. Mr Swanson's son had come to see her this evening — he'd booked under an assumed name. In all the time she'd had sex with him before the murder and being sectioned, he hadn't admitted to the familial relationship. He wasn't required to. She felt cheated, lied to, and wondered whether her mother had known but hadn't thought Miranda needed to know. And maybe she hadn't — after all, a customer was a customer, and as long as he paid, who cared who he was?

But he'd confessed tonight, **after** *they'd had sex (which was a calculated decision because he probably knew she wouldn't want to see him again afterwards). He'd said that because this was his first night with her* *since she'd started working again, he reckoned he ought to be upfront. She felt violated to be honest, like he was some kind of pervert who'd used the same pair of prostitutes as his father—the son had also had sex with Mum on a couple of occasions. It bothered her after his declaration, something incestuous about it didn't sit right, and she'd told him not to come back.*

His parting words still bothered her. "I'll come back if I want to, and I'll knock on the front door while I'm at it."

So now she contemplated changing her business model, adapting to the threat so that it no longer had any effect on her. If she wasn't having sex in the house, he could knock on the front door all he liked, because she'd loudly tell him to go away so the nosy neighbours could hear her. If he said, just as loudly, that he wanted to use her for sex, she'd tell him he'd made a mistake and that it was her mother he was after and she was dead, so there was no chance of him getting what he wanted. She'd speak to her other customers and ask them if they'd mind picking her up somewhere in a car.

The house was out of bounds.

More settled now she'd come to a decision, she composed the text in her head, memorising it so she could tap it into her phone tomorrow and send it en masse. At last, she drifted off to sleep, oddly excited about this new direction, and it wouldn't be for long because she'd only service the men until she'd met her monetary goal, then she'd embark on her new journey.

<hr>

The majority of the men were up for the change, a couple of them stating it would be more exciting to fuck her in the car anyway. She'd chosen a quiet street for them to collect her from, one lined with trees, no houses around for snooping people to take any notice of what was going on. Surprisingly, the sessions were over quicker than they were at home, probably because the punters were more excited about the possibility of getting caught. She supposed that with the absence of a bed there was no excuse to lounge around—with no home comforts there was no point in prolonging their sessions.

She had one more week to go and then she'd have enough money.

Then something unexpected happened—not unexpected in that she was naïve enough to think this kind of thing never occurred, but the fact that she'd got into a car with a stranger who'd stopped on the off chance that she was a working girl. She'd never done something so spontaneous before, nor so dangerous, but it had gone well, and he'd paid her what she'd asked for plus a tip.

It wasn't long before she was entertaining more passing motorists in between her booked clients. She had surpassed the hundred thousand goal. She had no more reason to be standing out here in the cold, in a remote spot, because she had reached the date where she'd told all of her original men she'd no longer be available. Instead, she played a game of standing in the darkness and seeing how many people stopped in the span of a six-hour evening.

Then she got bolder and searched news articles to try and find out where sex workers were standing these days — the good old British public writing in to complain about the tone being brought down by 'unsavoury' goings-on. She found one that mentioned an industrial estate so rocked up there one night, got friendly with some of the women, and secured herself a nice little earning spot.

She changed the subject every time Bunty asked her about the university course. This game was more exciting than she'd imagined, it gave her a thrill, and at the same time she was safe in between clients while she stood and chatted to the other women.

But then some of those women started to go missing. The police turned up to talk to Miranda and the others, as did journalists, and the general consensus was that they ought to stop working there, it was too dangerous.

For once, Miranda decided to take notice, and she found a new spot around the corner from The Angel, outside the graveyard. She'd be okay there.

Chapter Seventeen

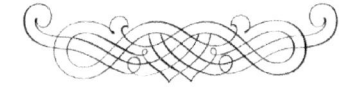

Cobden Road was full of skinny properties with an air of tiredness about them. Moody knew how they felt. He was knackered himself but wasn't about to turn down money for work from the twins. The homes were red-brick affairs with a blackened look that spoke of the days when London was full of dark smog that clung to everything. A good power washer would tart these places right up.

He'd parked the stolen Hyundai outside number six and sat there for a bit, checking the street for nosy neighbours as well as watching Shawnee's nan's house for anyone watching him through the voile curtains. All was quiet bar a couple of kids kicking a football to each other across the road, their hairlines sweaty where they'd been at it for a while. It brought back memories of childhood, when life had been so much simpler. He couldn't wait to grow up, and now he had, he wished he'd stayed a kid for a bit longer.

George had sent Moody some photos of Shawnee's diary confession, just so he knew what he was dealing with. He skim-read them now, and he had to give it to the girl, she had a good head on her shoulders to have thought up all this bollocks. When he got to the date that she'd committed the murder, he could see it all in his head as he read along. She'd been fucking savage.

According to the other intel he'd received, the nan, Isla Wetherby, had been a widow since nineteen ninety-two who'd lived alone since her husband had died of a heart attack. She worked three days a week at the Co-op round the corner and was in her sixties. Shawnee's mother had died of cancer last year, her father's whereabouts unknown, so Isla was all Shawnee had left. Surely she'd be the first port of call in a storm?

So he was fully prepared, Moody opened Facebook to see if Isla was on there. He found her quickly. She posted often. Selfies on nights out with her 'girls' who appeared to all be around the same age as her. Advice to her followers about where to get a freebie or something for cheap, usually from Home Bargains or B&M. She sold a lot of stuff, always under the header HAVING A CLEAR OUT [WINK EMOJI], but the items looked new, and he'd bet his last quid this shit was stolen.

Shawnee hadn't fallen far from the tree. Had her mother also been a wrong 'un?

He had a look at a few more pictures of Isla to try and get her measure. White. Platinum-blonde pixie cut. Fake tan. Turkey teeth, or they could be dentures. Not many wrinkles, so maybe she'd had surgery or Botox. She was someone who liked to drink and have a good time, that much was obvious, not to mention enjoying the finer things in life if the items in the background of some photos were anything to go by. She had mirrored furniture and crystal this and that—vases, bowls, trees with birds on the branches, roses, dogs, and cats.

He nosed through old uploaded photos. One with Isla, a woman who looked very much like her but younger, and a dark-skinned girl had the caption: *Three generations. Me, my daughter, and my granddaughter!* Some of the comments mentioned sadness at the loss of the daughter. Others bayed for the blood of Shawnee's father, saying he ought to step up now she didn't have a mother, one of them calling him a black cunt.

Fuck me, that's below the belt.

Moody got out of the car, pocketing his phone. His instructions were to bring Isla in if she refused to help. He approached the front door and tapped on the glass with his knuckle, the sound deadened by his leather gloves. He'd put on a zip-up sports coat to give him ease of movement in case he had to carry her to the car—whether she was awake or unconscious when he did that would depend on how she behaved. You never know, he might let her walk under her own steam.

The door opened, and she stood there in lilac Lycra leggings and a vest top, her chest and arms glistening with sweat, her hair damp and flat. "What do you want? You've interrupted my aerobics on YouTube."

"I've come to buy one of the electric toothbrushes you've got on your page."

She narrowed her eyes at him, assessing. "Who put you on to me?"

"I just saw the post because of that thing, People You May Know."

"Fuck me, I must remember to put my page to private. I keep forgetting. Hang on, I'll go and get one. Blue, pink, or black?"

"Black."

She spun away to go down the hall past a door, then a blingy mirror on the right hanging over a console table with some of that crystal shit on top. As soon as she was past the mirror and wouldn't catch his reflection to know he was following her, he went inside, and when she turned right, he quietly closed the door.

He did a bit of assessing of his own. Stairs to his left. Ahead, another door, closed.

He found her in a room that may once have been a small dining area but now contained shelves full of boxes around the edges and racking in the centre that held more boxes and some baskets containing shower gel, shampoo and the like, as if she ran a food bank but only dealt in stuff for personal hygiene. The boxes were another matter. Toothbrushes, shavers, hair dryers, straighteners, hoovers, screwdrivers. Had she robbed Argos or what?

She still hadn't noticed he'd come after her. She selected a black toothbrush box and, with her back to him, paused as though she'd finally sensed him there. Or could she smell his Dior Sauvage?

"I've got cameras in here," she said. "So if you're thinking of nicking off me, no sooner have you done it than I'll have your mug plastered on Facebook and Instagram. People around here won't take too kindly to someone ripping me off, not when I'm the equivalent of Robin Hood, so if I were you, I'd fuck off now and we'll say no more about it."

"I'm here on behalf of The Brothers."

Her shoulders sagged, and she turned to look at him, the box pressed to her chest. "I suppose I've had a good run. Twenty years I've been doing this and not paying any protection money.

Have they worked out how much I owe and sent you to collect it?"

"I expect they'll ignore any missed payments from the past if you tell them what they want to know."

"I'm not a grass. I'd rather pay the money."

"Trust me, you're better off being a grass."

She puffed out a sigh. "Did you really want this toothbrush or was that bollocks?"

"I could do with one, and can I have a pink one an' all for the missus?"

"They're twenty each."

"I wasn't expecting them for free." He took his wallet out of his pocket and handed her the money.

She took it and gave him the box. "I suppose you're going to want to *chat*."

"Yep."

He braced himself in case she swivelled round with a mind to whack him in the face with the pink box. Instead, she held it down by her side and scooted round him to stand in the doorway.

"If there's anything else you want in here, bring it into the kitchen with you once you've had a root round. Like I said, there's cameras, so I can see what you're up to."

She went to leave, but he called her back.

"Stay in here with me. I really don't need you doing a runner."

"I didn't plan to, I'm scared of no fucker, but whatever."

A wedge of white carrier bags hung from a hook on one of the centre shelving units, and he used one like a basket to do his shopping. She watched, leaning against the doorframe with her arms folded, probably totting up the prices in her head. He picked out a few bits of makeup for his bird—she'd be well chuffed because it was that expensive brand she always said she wanted but didn't have the money for. These were being sold for a tenner apiece rather than fifty. He reckoned she'd like those straighteners, too, the GHD brand. By the time he'd finished, he had four full bags.

"Are you done?" she asked.

"I think so."

"That's three hundred for that little lot as opposed to over six. You'd better have cash on you, because I don't run a tab here, nor do I take card payments."

He assumed she was a professional thief, or maybe she ran a gang of them. He was surprised he hadn't heard about her before, but then communities kept people like Isla close to their chests. They were a treasure to be protected if they could save you money, especially if they stole to order. She was probably well busy at Christmas.

He placed the bags on the floor and took an envelope out of his jacket pocket, counting out the cash and passing it over. He was getting lax — the envelope was from the last bonus George had paid him that he hadn't even taken out to put in his safe at home.

He followed her into a kitchen at the front. He assumed the living room spanned the back behind that closed door. He popped his bags on the floor by the washing machine, and at her gesture, sat at an island made out of an eight-cube unit on its side with a nice rectangle of polished wood on top, something he'd seen on the IKEA hack group on Facebook. He watched and read all kinds of shit while he was on jobs for the twins where there was a lot of sitting around.

She took a couple of Diet Cokes out of the fridge and pushed a can across the island to him. She kept away from him, leaning her backside against the sink unit, popping her can tab and taking a long swig. "So you're advising me to be a grass, which means if I'm not, I'll be in serious trouble with the twins."

"That's about it, yes." He opened his can and sipped.

"Go on then, ask me what you need to ask."

"Have you seen Shawnee recently?"

Isla frowned. "Not for a couple of weeks, and even then it was down the Swan on quiz night. She popped in for a drink, give me a quick hug and chatted for a minute, then she was off again. Is she okay?"

"We assume so. She was last seen legging it from her house when the twins paid her a visit. All right, she probably didn't know it was the twins, they're in disguise more often than not these days, but still, if you're running then it tends to point them to the fact you're up to no good."

"Or she was scared. Can you imagine having those two lumps coming to your front door? Just the size of them alone would have made her crap herself."

"Do you know what she's been doing recently?"

"In the pub, she said she'd been taking a break from her cleaning business, helping a mate out instead by housesitting for him."

"What she was actually doing was taking over his life—his house, his business, stealing his money. After she'd killed him."

Isla's mouth dropped open—she'd gone the whole hog had had her bottom teeth done nice, too. "You what? You're kidding me, aren't you? Shawnee wouldn't kill anyone. Well, not unless they were attacking her and she had to defend herself."

"By her own written confession, she murdered a drug dealer with a metal pole, wrapped him up in clingfilm, and stuffed him inside a punchbag—obviously she took the stuffing out of the bag first."

"I gathered that, but I don't believe you, not Shawnee."

"Would you like to see the pictures of the things she wrote on her laptop about it?"

Isla pushed her arse off the cupboard, put her Coke down, and approached the island with her hand out. Moody found the relevant images then gave her his phone. She read the screen, squinting to see, then pinching it to enlarge it, swiping side to side to read each line now that the image had been blown up. She genuinely appeared to not know what her granddaughter had been up to. Lifting her hand to her mouth, she shook her head, and the tears that had been bulging broke free to roll down her over-tanned cheeks. She pinched the screen to minimise it and then scrolled to the next image, repeating the process, clearly dumbfounded by what had been written.

Sometimes, Moody hated his job. There were days when he had to wreck someone's life, and this was one of them. Wasn't it weird how when you got up in the morning, you thought you knew what direction the next few hours we're going to go in, but then someone else swept in and ruined it. Isla had probably thought about nothing today except aerobics on YouTube and selling a few things out of her little shop, yet here he was, ripping that to shreds. He enjoyed what he did for the most part, even beating people up because it released a lot of internal anger he'd stored from being a kid, but people like this woman here, he didn't like being the bearer of bad news.

Still, it paid the bills.

"If you swipe to the one dated Friday the sixteenth of August, twenty twenty-four…"

She did that, and Moody sipped his drink while he waited for her to digest the words describing the murder. God knew what was going through her mind, poor cow. If he were in her shoes, he'd be remembering Shawnee as a small girl, an innocent who'd never dream of killing someone. A cheeky smile, a burbling brook of laughter, maybe a kind heart. Or had she been a little devil? He'd ask himself how she'd got where she had and whether her mother dying had played a big factor in her decision-making. Had her absent father shaped who she was today? Was her nan her only anchor?

When Isla had finished, she placed the phone on the island and shoved it away from her as if she couldn't bear to have it anywhere near her. More tears fell, and she backed away to the cupboard again, grabbing her can and draining it dry. A sob moved her chest up and down, and she blew out through pursed lips, the exhalation shaky.

"That might not have been written by Shawnee," she said.

"True, but it was her laptop, so it's highly likely. I can understand why you'd say that, though. It's hard to think of someone you love being anyone other than who you thought they were."

"I'd swear down she didn't have it in her to commit murder, but now… People change as they grow up, and maybe she hid her true self from me all this time."

"Do you know Scott Talbert?"

"Yes. Those two have known each other since they were kids when they went to nursery together, then to primary and secondary." She stared at nothing and smiled—seeing memories inside her head? "He always followed her around—she was the bossy one, the one in charge. I can see her getting him to do something like this, well, the stealing Andre's money part, not killing him. She takes after me in that she'll put her hand to anything if it means making money. Between me and you, she started a cleaning business just so she could steal things from the houses once she'd got the trust of the people she worked for. If they accused her of anything, she gaslit them and told them they must have misplaced it. She never stole from the same person twice, so they believed her explanation."

"If you're not a grass, why tell me this?"

"Because I need you to know that's all Shawnee is. A scam artist, not a killer."

"As you can understand, the twins want to know where she is."

"I wouldn't tell you if I knew, but I actually don't know."

He believed her. "So if I leave and she comes here hoping you'll hide her, would you?"

She wiped her cheeks with her palms. "Of course I fucking would, she's my granddaughter."

"Then I'm going to have to ask you to come with me to see the twins."

"So they can have a *word* with me themselves to change my mind, make me dob my own family in?"

"It might be more than a word, and it's in your best interests to grass Shawnee up, much as you don't want to. Family or not, she made a decision that means she blipped on the twins' radar, so now she has to pay the consequences."

Isla took a deep breath and then blew it out, shaking her hands and arms as though gearing herself up for a boxing match. "Right, then we'd better go, hadn't we."

Chapter Eighteen

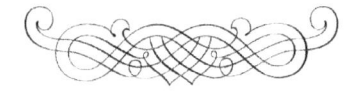

Puggy stood and smiled at the kitchen. It was lovely and clean now, only the floor to go. Miss Daulton was going to think he'd done so well when he told her he'd scrubbed it himself. He had to remember to say that to her, because it was a big secret that Shawnee was here, and no one could know she'd done it. It was odd that she'd come here without any boxes, though. She'd never come without them before, and he was due a delivery.

"Will the courier bring the boxes?" he asked her.

She was on the floor scraping along the lino where it met the bottom of the cupboards. It was a bit scummy, a few Rice Krispies stuck to the honey he'd dropped that time. It was black from dirt now.

"You're not going to be needed to sell the baggies anymore," she said. "Andre's no longer dealing."

That was weird. Andre had been dealing for a long time, Fish and Chips had told him that, and Puggy couldn't imagine not doing it anymore now he'd got used to the pocket money. He had a special phone with a list of customers on it, and when the new stuff came in, he let them know so they could come and get it. Sometimes the buyers stopped and chatted to him for a bit, and it was great because it felt like he had friends.

"Do Fish and Chips know it's not happening anymore?" he asked.

"Andre will send them a message."

When Fish had punched Puggy the other day, it had been because Puggy hadn't let him know a new batch of boxes had arrived—and neither had Andre. Fish had said he was sick of being left out of the loop and he was going to get hold of Andre and tell him to stuff his job up his arse. He also said Fish and Chips were too busy to be coming round to Puggy's to babysit him when it came down to making sure nobody had scammed him of more drugs than they'd paid for. He reckoned it was a pain in the arse to check the notebook Puggy kept that showed who'd bought what against what was left in the boxes. Nobody ever tried to get Puggy to give them more, so he didn't understand why Fish and Chips even needed to come. He supposed that meant Andre didn't trust him. Or could it be that he didn't trust the customers? Fish had said something about Puggy being thick and needing to be protected.

"I'll miss the money," he said.

"I'll miss mine, too. You know, for handing the boxes over and delivering some to you."

"How come Andre's stopping?"

"He's gone back to Italy."

Puggy pinched his bottom lip. "I'm going to have to tell the customers on my phone not to come here anymore."

"Yeah, your last box will almost have run out by now."

She was ever so clever, knowing that when Andre usually kept details of his business to himself. Or he always had with Puggy anyway.

"How come you knew that?" he asked.

She stopped scraping to look up at him. "Because Andre put me in charge of distribution, which means I had to keep an eye on who needed a new delivery and when."

"Ah."

She reached for the dustpan and brush to sweep up the mess, then stood and tapped the bits into the bin. "I'll sweep and mop the floor in here, and then we'll move on to the living room, so if you want to go and look for that unit on Argos, I can order it to be delivered."

He shuffled off, closing the door behind him—he didn't like the noise of the hoover. In his bedroom, he locked himself in and took his phone out. It was best he let Fish and Chips know that Andre didn't need them to babysit him anymore. If he told them on the phone then they wouldn't come here again, but if he waited for them to turn up at his flat and *then* told them, it meant he'd see them, and he didn't want to.

He didn't like Fish, even though he'd said sorry for getting angry with him last time. He'd muttered something about not hitting disabled people and that he should be ashamed of himself, but fuck, Puggy was such an annoying little twat.

Puggy had pretended not to hear that. He'd pretended it hadn't hurt.

He brought up the WhatsApp group and tapped in a message.

―――

The hoover had stopped making that horrible noise, so Puggy left his bedroom to find Shawnee. She was putting the hoover and the mop and bucket away in the cupboard in the hallway.

"Did you pick out a unit?" she asked and closed the cupboard door.

"I forgot. You pick one."

She took her phone out and scrolled for a while, then showed him a nice white shoe cupboard. He nodded, and she smiled.

"Okay, that will arrive tomorrow," she said. "You can help me put it together if you want."

"It might be too hard for me."

"We'll figure it out between us. Have you decided what you want for dinner? It's a bit early yet, but we could have our lunch and dinner combined."

"Pizza."

"Okay, what do you want on it?"

"Pepperoni and ham and onion and sweetcorn and…some chips."

She used her phone again. "Right, that's sorted. Are all the clothes on the floor in the living room dirty?"

"Yeah."

"Let's pick it all up then and take it into the kitchen."

A few minutes later, she was sorting it into piles of light and dark and explaining to him why he couldn't mix them in the machine. "You've done really well to keep on top of it by yourself as there's only three piles here, so we'll stick one on to wash while we clean the living room."

"It's too hard for me." He'd found if he said something was too hard, he often didn't have to do it.

"Then you can sit and watch telly while I do it."

She popped a pile of washing into the machine, found the liquid pods Miss Daulton had told him to buy—for some reason she'd said he mustn't eat them, even though they looked like big Haribo sweets—and then she filled the sink with hot water, putting in another of the pods.

"What are you doing that for?"

"I need to soak your boxer shorts, okay?"

"Okay."

"Do you have a lot of accidents?"

Puggy didn't want to talk about that. Miss Daulton was all right when it came to personal stuff, but not Shawnee. "Can you clean the living room now?"

She scooped up the pile of boxer shorts and pushed them beneath the soapy water, then rinsed her hands and dried them on a tea towel. "You carry the roll of black bags for me, and I'll take the cleaning spray and cloths."

He liked the way she explained what they were going to do next instead of just doing it. He preferred to know what was coming. Surprises weren't his thing, which was why he was unsettled when she'd turned up at his door earlier. But it was okay, it was nice to have her here, and the kitchen was clean and soon the living room would be, and so would his underpants. Maybe she'd stay for a long time and look after him. He could hide her from the nasty men and wouldn't be so lonely. Because it *would* be lonely now he wasn't going to have people coming to buy the baggies.

He walked down the hallway behind her, and someone knocked on the front door.

"Is that the pizza here already? That was quick," Shawnee said.

He turned to see two shapes behind the glass in the front door.

Oh no. He'd told them not to come, but they'd done it anyway.

Fish and Chips were here.

Puggy swallowed tightly. "Shawnee, I think you need to go and hide in the cupboard."

Chapter Nineteen

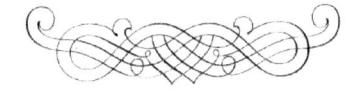

From what Miranda could see from her spot outside the graveyard, there were no CCTV cameras. She quickly glanced at the nearby houses—a couple of video doorbells, but other than that she was free and clear to go about her business. Even if she was filmed getting into a car, no one could prove what she was

getting in there for. There wasn't outright proof that she was selling sex.

A pinch of guilt twisted in her stomach. She could become known as the lady who sullied this part of the estate, the one good girls turned their noses up at or fretted that she was there to steal their men, luring them into infidelity. Plus she was supposed to have made contact with the twins. She was working right around the corner from a pub they visited often, which was rude as fuck. She'd get hold of them later via the lady at The Angel. She'd have to pay them a cut of her money, which was annoying but necessary if she didn't want to upset them.

Then again, if she was unlikely to get caught, why should she?

Could she take the risk?

She stood in front of the locked cemetery gates. She hadn't dressed as provocatively as she usually would, given that she was on a housing estate, but bar having a neon sign above her head, she reckoned it was obvious enough what she was doing to those who were looking for it, who she was, and what was on offer. For those not in the know, she'd probably come across as some woman waiting for her mates or a boyfriend.

An SUV went past, so she wrote off that chance to pick someone up. She doubted she'd get lucky the first time, and besides, at the industrial estate, a lot of men drove by without stopping, checking the women out first before coming back later, maybe after they'd given themselves a pep talk and found the courage to approach.

She tapped her foot, impatient, although she knew the score by now. Men would come prowling eventually. Wasn't the wait the part of the thrill she liked the best? The anticipation of whether she'd get a customer or not?

An engine rumbled, and the SUV came back and stopped, the passenger window going down to reveal a youngish bloke with a ready smile. He didn't look the type. He was pretty tasty so probably had his pick of women, but then did he? She was judging a book by its cover. He could be bricking it inside, a low-confidence kind of person.

"Are you…?" He didn't sound sure how he should phrase it. Was he nervous? Was this his first time?

As though her intuition had been on holiday, it came back with a whoosh, and she remembered that an SUV had been used to collect those three women who'd gone missing from the industrial estate. But there were loads of SUVs, and anyway, as far as she could recall, this one's number plate was completely different.

He looked too nice to be nasty, so she stepped closer.

"What are you after?"

"Just to drive around and a chat to be honest. Is that something you do?"

Bless him, he was definitely nervous, and she felt sorry for him now.

She shook her head. "Not really, no, although some people do chat afterwards, but they have to pay me extra for it. I can't say I've ever just *chatted."*

"There's a first time for everything, so the saying goes. How much do you charge?"

"A hundred for whatever, no exceptions."

His eyes shot wider, and it was clear he was a novice at this. "Christ, so if someone just wanted a blow job, that would end up being pretty expensive."

She shrugged. "Not my problem. Fixed rates, end of. Your chat will also cost you a hundred, just so we're clear on that."

She wasn't about to tell him this, but if she didn't have her self-imposed tariff she'd have actually done it cheaper for him, considering how nice-looking he was and the way she got butterflies when he made eye contact with her. But she did *have a tariff and she wasn't going to budge on it.*

"How long do you need to chat for?" she asked.

"Half an hour?"

"What about?"

"The missus, of course."

That old chestnut. "Doesn't she understand you?"

He grinned. "Something like that."

"How did I know you were going to say that?"

"Maybe because I'm a walking cliché. Listen, I'm new to this, so can you cut me some slack? I don't generally go around picking women up, but you look nice, so…"

"Aww, trying to soft-soap me, are you?"

"Nope. So are you up for it or what?"

She sensed she was pushing it too far. She'd lose the sale if she continued teasing him when he clearly wasn't used to chatting with women in this way. She shrugged again and got in the front with him. Popped her seat belt on. He drove away through the estate.

"Do you mind if I park round the back of Tony's Tiles?" he asked.

She raised her eyebrows. "On the industrial *estate? Where those* women *went missing? Do you actually* want *to become a suspect? I mean, you've already got the SUV…"*

He glanced across and frowned at her. "What do you mean, women going missing?"

Was he being serious? It seemed so, considering he appeared confused, but she'd imagined everybody in London would have heard about those women by now.

"Have you been living under a rock? It's all over the news and social media."

"I've been working away and only just got back today."

"What, you haven't even been to see your missus yet and already you want to slag her off to me?"

"Actually, we'll just keep driving," he said, ignoring her question.

Was that a red flag? Was the topic of his missus, even though he'd asked to talk about her, a difficult one for him to dive into?

"Do me a favour and indulge my kink," he said. "There's a blindfold in the glove box. Stick it on, will you?"

He'd said it so casually she didn't feel uncomfortable with the request. It wasn't the weirdest one she'd had, but to put one on while she was at home was a different matter to being in the car with a stranger. He seemed all right, nice enough, but that's what all people said after they'd got away from a serial killer. Was she on her way to being one of those people, or would she be unlucky and not be able to get away should he suddenly change and go weird on her?

"Err, so you get off on talking to women who have a blindfold on?"

"Yep. It takes all sorts to make a world."

"Hmm." She gave him the quick once-over. No weird vibes coming from him. No gut instinct telling her not to do it. Fuck it, she reached into the glove box and took the blindfold out, slipping it over her eyes. "Okay, so talk to me." She folded her arms over her boobs so he couldn't cop a sneaky feel. They'd agreed on just a chat, and once an agreement was made, there was no going back or changing minds.

He told her about his missus, although she wasn't really his missus. She was the one who'd got away, the one he could have had if he'd played his cards better, except he hadn't, and now he was regretting his life without her.

"I regret a lot of things actually."

"Don't we all?" she said.

"Have you ever had a special someone?" he asked.

She snorted. God, if only he knew what she'd been through. "I haven't exactly had the chance."

"Sounds like there's a story there."

"One I'm not about to tell."

"Go on. It might do you good to get it off your chest."

True. She gave him a quick rundown—basically that she was alone in the world with no one to give a shit about her, although there was Bunty, but she didn't mention her. Then there was Alicia and Val, who would give a toss if she let them, but again, she didn't bother telling him about them. To all intents and purposes she was *alone, she only had herself to rely on.*

There was something to be said about talking to someone in the dark. She couldn't distract herself by looking at anything, and the blackness created by the blindfold gave her a comforting void to sink into where she just spoke and spoke without interruption. It also meant she had to focus on what subjects her mind presented to her. It was different to when she'd had to speak to a psychiatrist. At least with this bloke she didn't have to pretend she wasn't a prostitute.

"I'd better take you back," he said. "Keep the blindfold on until we get to the graveyard, though."

They talked about all sorts on the way back, mundane stuff—the weather, the cost of living—and she found herself liking him enough to ask his name.

"Mocha," he said. "Like the drink."

"That's an unusual nickname."

"I suppose so. What would yours be if you had to have one?"

"Pearl."

"Why's that? Any particular reason?"

"Pearls represent prosperity, don't they?" She circled a finger near her face to indicate the fake pearl

nose stud, then she fiddled with the ones in her earlobes. She'd own real ones one day.

"Hmm. I'd pick a fuck-off expensive watch myself, but each to their own."

She laughed, surprised to be so content in his company that she'd let her guard down enough to do that. It had taken her ages to warm up to Alicia and Val. It had taken less time for her to open up to Mocha than it had with them, but maybe because she'd picked at her open wounds with her Ward F friends it made it easier to do the same with him. Whatever, it was nice to feel so safe.

The weird thought came into her head then that maybe she'd regret thinking that one day, how she felt safe with him and maybe she shouldn't. She froze for a second, holding her breath and going through their conversation to find anything there that she should be alarmed about. There was nothing, so it was her own paranoia talking, although Val would say it was survival instinct giving her a little nudge.

She moved her hand to lift the blindfold.

"Can you keep it on just for a bit longer?"

She stretched her arm out to feel for the door handle, another alarm bell jangling quietly. A just-in-case tinkle. "Why?"

"I don't want you to see my mum's house. Not saying you'd do this, but if you turn up unexpectedly, she'll get the wrong end of the stick and start picking out wedding dresses, know what I mean?"

She laughed again. God, she was just being silly, overly cautious. This bloke was no more a serial killer then she was Doris Day.

"How far until the graveyard?" she asked.

"Couple of minutes."

"You'd best keep talking to get your money's worth."

"It was good chatting to you. You're a nice bird. It's just a shame… I had to pick you, you have to understand that. I had no choice."

Her stomach rolled over, and she snatched the blindfold off, staring out of the windscreen. Headlights picked out what looked like a tarmac road with grass either side. Ahead, presenting as a shadow, stood what she reckoned was a big house.

"Err, if you don't want me to see your mum's gaff, why are we here, and why did you have to pick me? What are you going on about? Look, just take me back to The Angel and I won't say any more about it. You don't even have to pay me."

"I wasn't planning to anyway. You're not allowed your own money."

"What?" she said while looking at him and yanking the door handle at the same time.

"The only advice I'd give you is do as you're told and everything might be okay."

Might? She felt sick, and dread flooded her system. The bloody door wouldn't open! Fuck!

"Please, let me out of here."

"I can't. I wish I could, but seriously, I can't."

She stopped struggling with the door—it was fucking pointless anyway—and worked out in her head whether she could clamber between the front seats in time and get in the back to escape that way. Then again, he probably had the child locks on.

"Those women," he said, "from the industrial estate."

Oh God…

"They're dead. I had to kill them. They were too hot to handle." He blew out a long breath. "Listen to me, do whatever you're told, pretend to like it, and then maybe one day you'll be allowed to go home, but for now, you have to stay here for a while, all right?"

Her mind flickered back to her time in Ward F. Six weeks of continuous time away from her house was allowed. She didn't go out much, and she'd stopped the Saturday morning shopping sprees anyway, so it was rare that she saw anyone in her street unless Bunty nipped in. The nosy neighbours might think she'd gone all reclusive again if they didn't see her about. But there was Bunty. What if she got worried after Miranda didn't respond to any texts or knocks on the front door? At least the police would be alerted that Miranda had gone missing. She wasn't about to tell Mocha that, though. She had a horrible feeling that if she mentioned she had a kindly neighbour, then something bad might happen.

"Get it into your head that this is your home now." He stopped outside a large house with shutters on the windows.

The front door opened, and another man stood there. He came towards the vehicle, the light from the headlamps giving her a good view of him. He looked a bit sick to his stomach, to be honest, which didn't make sense if he was in on this crap. Unless he was used to Mocha bringing women home and he knew what was about to go on and didn't like it. Or perhaps he was the engineer behind it all, and Mocha warning her to do as she was told was because of this fella.

"What the fuck?" She stared at Mocha. "What the hell are you going to do to me?"

"Me? Nothing if you behave. But if you don't, then I'll have to hurt you."

Chapter Twenty

Fish and Chips, aka the Unidenticals, Noel and Joel, parked outside Andre's house, incensed the bastard wasn't answering his mobile, which meant they'd had to come round here, something they'd never done before. All of their communication had been done over the phone, and payment had been left in a hole in a tree round the corner from their lock-up. If they had to go round Puggy's, Andre sent a message. They were never told anything through a third party, so it was annoying they'd had to hear about this shit because of one.

If Puggy was to be believed, Andre was shutting up shop, which was all well and good because Noel and Joel didn't need the money and nor did they need to keep popping in on Puggy who got right on Noel's nerves. There was something about him that boiled his piss. Noel had committed what their mother would say was a cardinal sin when he'd punched him in the face that time. You weren't meant to pick on those who didn't have all their faculties, but fucking hell, Puggy had caught him on a bad day. Still, that was no excuse.

He adjusted the balaclava, not giving a shit that the posh neighbours would see him and his twin with their faces covered in black wool, making it obvious that they might be up to no good, but he was fucked if he'd show his mug. He'd rather it be assumed they were bad men than have them recognised later down the line. Because they weren't in the know about what had been going on with Andre for him to want to give up dealing, it was best their identity remained a secret so they didn't get caught up in any mess.

They got out of the stolen car with the doctored number plates and went up the steps, bashing on the front door and calling out Andre's name through the letterbox. With no answer, and no inclination to stick around only to keep knocking like a knob, Noel nudged his brother for them to leave.

A short, shrill scream brought his attention to a house three doors down, a blonde woman standing on her steps clutching one of those rat dogs that yipped and yapped at her distress. Taking the balaclava off would possibly shut her up immediately, but he wasn't going to risk his face popping up on numerous camera doorbells. For all he knew, the people who lived here were suspicious of people turning up to Andre's door, and who knew whether they were secretly keeping an eye on the comings and goings for the Old Bill.

"It's not what it seems," he called out to her, a hand up in an attempt to placate. "We've come to play a joke on Andre. Pretend to rob him an' that, but he isn't in."

She quieted, stroking her dog to either calm it or herself. "Rob him? What a ghastly trick. He's…he's on holiday in Italy, and his cousins have been helping some big men deep clean the house. They came in a little white van."

A little white van. Noel didn't glance at his brother; he didn't have to, to know that Joel would have also made the connection. Andre had supposedly stopped dealing, he'd supposedly gone to Italy, and cleaning men had come to go through his house. Fuck, he must have been killed in there. The Brothers must have found out what he was up to. Or was it just a coincidence and the van belonged to someone else?

"Did you catch the company name, love?" Noel asked.

"It just said Cardigan Cleaning or something like that."

Any number of people could have chosen that, but Noel still had the jitters.

"These cousins," he said. "What did they look like?"

"Italian. Black hair, sunglasses, expensive clothes."

"Men?"

"No, women."

"Cheers for your help."

They got in the car, Joel driving, and didn't speak until they'd parked up in an area by a row of garages. Andre going back to Italy reminded Noel of working for Tommy Coda and having to babysit—well, threaten—that Leanora bitch they'd had to look after for him, the French tart, which then reminded him of Puggy and how they always seemed to end up babysitting people, getting paid to make sure they were doing as they were told.

Noel was sick of it.

"What now?" Joel asked.

"First, we ditch this motor in case that blonde woman phones the police on us, then we go and see Puggy to find out where he got his information from, then we find ourselves another job to replace the cash we're losing from Andre."

They did so many bits and bobs for people that they were never short of cash, so losing Andre's wasn't a big deal, but Noel had always promised to make sure Joel never went without, so he felt it was his responsibility to ensure they always had a steady stream of work on the go.

"I'm not upset we won't have to go and see Puggy anymore," Joel said.

"Me neither."

"Believe it or not, I didn't like being paid to bully him."

Noel sighed. "Same, but at least you didn't get annoyed and hit him."

"He was pushing your buttons. He'd push anyone's."

"Not an excuse. Anyway, let's go."

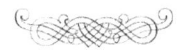

Joel came to a stop outside the block of flats to watch what was going on at Puggy's door. Two food delivery men chatted to Puggy who held a couple of pizza boxes and a brown paper bag. That was the trouble with Puggy, he kept people talking, people who were too polite to tell him to fuck off because it was obvious he had a disability or two, but it wasn't like the kid didn't know what he was doing. He was well aware there were drugs in those baggies, and in order to make money he had to sell them. He had a sly look to him sometimes where Noel swore he wasn't as thick as he made out.

The pizza men finally stepped away, Noel lowering his window so he could listen to their conversation as they walked past.

One of them told the other, "That customer is a prime example of what you need to avoid if you have a long list of deliveries on the same run. Wasting half an hour talking means the other pizzas will go cold, but at least today this delivery was the last of that particular run."

Noel assumed the second bloke was being trained, which explained why it had taken two men to bring food, something he'd wondered about as soon as they'd pulled up. His mind had gone to them being people who were going to rob the drugs Puggy stored in his cupboard, handing the pizzas over as a sweetener.

With that crisis averted—because Noel and Joel would have sorted the pizza men out if needed—they got out of the car, keeping their balaclavas on. People around here were so used to it they didn't take any notice. Fish and Chips were just the men who visited the bloke in the ground-floor flat.

At the front door, Joel knocked, Noel drumming his fingertips on his thigh, already frustrated at the thought of dealing with Puggy if he was in a particularly divvy mood. It took a while for the door to open, but there Puggy stood, red sauce either side of his mouth where he'd so obviously rammed a triangle of pizza in too far.

"Oh. It's you." Puggy closed the door a bit so he was peering at them through a four-inch gap. "I asked you not to come."

"Why's that? Got something to hide, have you?" Noel asked.

"I'm not hiding anything. I'm good at keeping secrets."

"What secret's that?"

"I don't know."

"You just said you were good at keeping secrets."

"Because I am."

"And I asked what secret it was."

Puggy's brain must have caught up with what he'd let slip. His face flamed red, and he stuck his tongue out to try and lick the sauce. "I'd better get back in."

"What's the rush?"

"My dinner's getting cold."

"What did you buy two pizzas for?"

Puggy thought about that for a moment. "Because I'm greedy."

"So it isn't because you've got someone in the flat?"

"There's no one in the flat. It's a secret."

This exchange was why Noel had got so shirty with him before. Half the time you couldn't have a proper conversation with the kid, and it was frustrating as fuck, but he reminded himself that hitting Puggy again would serve no purpose except to make Noel feel bad days down the line, heaping guilt on top of the guilt he already felt.

"Are you safe?" Joel asked.

It was the question Andre had asked them to pose to him if things seemed dodgy.

"Yes."

"Are you sure?"

"Yes. She won't hurt me."

"Who won't hurt you?" Noel asked.

"It's a secret."

"Does the secret have a name?"

Puggy glanced over his shoulder and then back to Noel and Joel, leaning forward to whisper, "Shawnee."

What was *she* doing there? If Andre wasn't dealing anymore, why had she come to deliver boxes? Or was that the last load Puggy would be getting? If so, that meant he still needed Noel and

Joel's protection, so why had Puggy told them they wouldn't be required anymore?

Noel had to get to the bottom of this or he'd go mental. "Did she bring boxes?"

"No, there aren't any more of those, but she bought me a shoe cupboard, that's coming tomorrow, and the pizzas, and she cleaned my kitchen. She's cleaning the living room after dinner, and then the bath after so I can get in it without the ring of scum."

Noel's stomach churned. "What's she doing all that for?"

"Because she likes cleaning and she's staying here for a bit. She's giving me money and buying takeaways."

"Do you know why she's staying here and not at her own place?"

"There's nasty men after her, but that's a secret an' all. You can't tell anyone. She can't know I told you because I promised I wouldn't."

The mention of nasty men was a worry, but considering they weren't being paid to look after Puggy anymore, it wasn't their problem, so Noel asked, "How did you find out Andre wasn't dealing anymore?"

"Shawnee told me."

Noel sniffed. "Right, well, see you around then."

They returned to the old banger they'd nicked, Joel driving towards the nearest pub, reading Noel's mind that he needed a fucking drink. They abandoned the car behind a high-rise, took their balaclavas off, and went to the Crown on foot, neither of them speaking, but Noel would guarantee Joel was thinking about the exchange with Puggy just as much as he was.

They walked into the pub and went straight to the bar, ordering a pint of lager each and chicken and chips in a basket. They sat at a table closest to the door to wait for their food to arrive, neither of them stupid enough to talk about Andre and the goings-on in here—too many listening ears.

A couple of the twins' men came in, the type who tended to ask questions and slip you fifty quid in an envelope if you gave them the right answer. Noel's suspicions rose. Considering cleaning men had been at Andre's, and Shawnee was hiding out at Puggy's, and now these men were here, something was definitely up. The men went round asking every customer a question, the majority of them shaking their heads. Then it was Noel and Joel's turn.

The one in the *Peaky Blinders* cap and a suit jacket with a watch fob and chain was shorter than his mate who had on a more modern suit and no hat.

"What's up?" Noel asked.

"Have you seen Shawnee Wetherby lately?" Peaky wanted to know.

"We haven't *seen* her, no," Joel said.

Noel thought about everything—what if Shawnee was hiding from the nasty men, The Brothers, because she'd shafted Andre and the twins were coming after her? With Puggy having such loose lips, it wouldn't be long before word got round that Fish and Chips had paid him a visit, and even though the kid didn't know they were really the Unidenticals, it still felt like too much of a spotlight would be on them. He nudged Joel who looked at him, raised his eyebrows, and nodded. A lot of the time they pretended they were The Brothers when they were out and about doing jobs in their balaclavas, so really they owed the blokes a favour for assuming their identities without permission.

"From what we were told, she's kipping round a flat." Noel gave them the address. "The bloke who lives there, he's got special needs." That was the only way he could put it so they didn't go in there all guns blazing and scare the shit out of Puggy.

"How old is this information?" Peaky asked.

Noel checked his watch. "Twenty minutes."

Peaky took an envelope out of his pocket and dropped it on the table. "Cheers."

The men walked out. Noel picked up the envelope, pleased they weren't in their local. No one knew them here, so being seen to take a payout, or basically being a grass or a Brothers supporter, wasn't a problem.

They ate their chicken and chips in silence.

Chapter Twenty-One

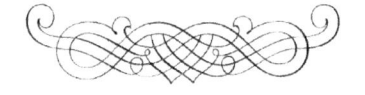

The work burner vibrated in George's pocket for long enough that it annoyed the shit out of him. He was out in the field by their house, walking their recently acquired dog, Ralph, a collie that had belonged to Tommy Coda's mum. Mother and son were no longer in the picture, and a vet willing to take a backhander and keep his mouth shut had removed the dog's microchip and put in a new one. Ralph now belonged to them and was a big part of the family. He sat on the sofa and watched telly with them, and the bugger had wormed his way into George's bedroom, where George had placed a big fluffy bed on the floor for him. He enjoyed his walks with Ralph, they helped to clear his mind of its churning clutter, but if the work burner was vibrating as much as it was then it meant something had kicked off and he'd better take a look.

Carling: Men in Crown said target is at the following address.

Carling: 2 Spalding Crescent.

Carling: Warning, man who lives in flat has special needs.

Carling: We're opposite the address now.

Carling: Will remain until you arrive.

If there was one thing that was guaranteed to piss George off, it was people who sent multiple text messages for every sentence instead of sending it in one big paragraph. No wonder his phone had been blowing up.

GG: Cheers.

On the way back home, Ralph trotting nicely on the lead beside him, George contemplated what to do next. Moody was at the warehouse with Shawnee's nan, so should they collect Shawnee and speak to the women at the same time or separately? Did the special needs angle play a part in this, or was it just a coincidence? He was well aware of how drug dealers, especially those in county lines, used vulnerable people to either store drugs or sell them, patsies who could take the blame should they get caught by the authorities. It had been on Shawnee's list to collect the gear, so it made sense that she'd go to the person she'd either persuaded or paid to keep them safe for her. Yes, a shitload had been found at Andre's house, but there could also be some at the flat.

George sent a message to Mason to find out who lived at Spalding Crescent.

Leaving the field and taking the lane that would lead directly to the back of the house, he jogged along, Ralph panting, and by the time he got indoors his phone had buzzed again. He read the message.

MASON: RENTED FROM THE COUNCIL TO AN EAMON PUGGLE, NINETEEN.

"Greg?" George poured fresh water in Ralph's bowl and placed it on the floor.

Because they were heading off shortly, George filled the automatic treat dispenser with kibble and a metal bowl with a can of wet food. Greg hadn't bothered answering but came into the kitchen with a towel around his waist.

"Did you see the messages?" George asked.

"No, I've been in the shower."

"Shawnee's apparently with some bloke in a flat." George explained what he thought had been going on as they went into the garage to put on new disguises. "We'll go and get her now, but we need to be careful how we handle the bloke."

Once George was ready, he returned to the kitchen to add more water to Ralph's bowl, shut the kitchen door that led to the hallway, and made sure the dog's bed was plumped up nice. He switched out the current toys for new ones so Ralph didn't get bored, kissed him on the head, and let him know they'd be back later. At the last second, he switched the radio on so Ralph wasn't lonely, then he got in the van and they were on their way.

Outside the block of flats, George and Greg took a moment to take in their surroundings. Six boys played football on the green in front of the high-rise. A part of George wished he and Greg had turned up here as The Brothers in their trademark suits and BMW, but out of respect for Jet and the embarrassment of her being tricked, they'd agreed to keep her involvement in this a secret. No mention of this would be made at any point in leader meetings—basically, none of this ever happened.

A woman pushing a buggy walked by. A kid in a tracksuit and baseball cap scuffed along behind her, earbuds in, phone in front of his face. Fuck having a teenager and a baby at the same time; it had to be a lot of hard work. A quick glance ahead, and George spotted Carling sitting in a car watching the flats.

GG: WE'RE HERE.

CARLING: NO MOVEMENT IN THE WHOLE TIME WE'VE BEEN HERE.

CARLING: TEZ CHECKED THE REAR OF THE FLATS.

CARLING: GROUND FLOOR HAVE GARDENS.

CARLING: GATES LEAD TO ALLEY.

GG: Cheers. Stay put, and for fucking fuck's sake, stop writing every sentence in separate messages. You're doing my tree in.

Carling: Sorry. I find bullet points are easier to take in.

GG: Well, I don't. Pack it the fuck in.

A fresh wave of irritation taking hold, George swerved his attention to Eamon's front door. A light had come on behind the glass, showing a couple of silhouettes moving around and then disappearing.

George held the messages out towards Greg. "The back is going to have to be watched while we're at the front. I'll get Carling and Tez to do it."

GG: Go round the back in case either of them try to leg it. Our plan is to take her, and if it's obvious the kid was coerced into being involved, we'll leave him be.

For now. George would revisit Eamon at a later date to see if there was anything they could do to help. If he was vulnerable, George didn't like the idea of leaving him open to other people taking advantage.

Carling and Tez got out of their car and disappeared down the side of the high-rise.

The burner phone buzzed.

CARLING: IN POSITION.

George waited for another bullshit sentence to appear, and when one didn't, he smiled, satisfied Carling had got the memo.

"Let's go," Greg said.

They left the van and walked to number two, George so conscious of the children on the green that he went back to the van, took money out of the envelopes in the glove box, and walked over to the kids.

"Do me a favour and fuck off for a bit." He handed each child twenty quid.

Every single one of them ran down an alley opposite that led to a parade of shops.

George returned to his brother, and they knocked on the door. A figure appeared at the end of what might be a hallway and vanished to the left. Then another came closer to the door, pausing for a moment, opening it.

The young man who stood there blinked at them, his bottom lip wet, his eyes watery as if he'd been crying. Was Shawnee being a bitch to him?

"Are you all right?" George asked.

"No."

"You look like you've been crying."

"I got told off for standing at the door and talking to the pizza men for too long, and then Fish and Chips came and I talked to them an' all."

"Who told you off?"

"I can't say, it's a secret, and you look like nasty men."

"Sorry about that. Can we speak to Shawnee, please?"

"How come you know she's here? No one's supposed to know."

"A little bird told us."

"Birds can't talk."

George smiled. "So can you go and get her for us?"

"Who?"

"Shawnee."

"I can't because she's not hiding in my cupboard. It's a secret."

George smiled again. "I'm going to ask you nicely to move out of the way because I don't want to have to *make* you, all right?"

"All right."

"Please will you move out of my way?"

"I can't let you in. No one can come in except Shawnee and Fish and Chips."

"Who are Fish and Chips?"

"Andre asks them to come here to make sure I'm okay. They wear balaclavas like the men on the telly who rob shops and stuff."

"And you say *we* look like nasty men," George joked.

Eamon didn't laugh. "You do."

"We need to ask Shawnee some questions about Andre, so either you go and get her, or we'll come in and find her."

"But she'll tell me off again, and if you're the nasty men and you take her away, no one's going to be here to put my shoe cupboard together when it arrives tomorrow."

"We'll send someone round to do it."

"Okay."

"Okay that someone can come and put your cupboard together, or okay that we can come in and see Shawnee? We won't let her tell you off anymore."

"Okay to both." Eamon shuffled to the side, squishing himself against the wall near piles of pizza boxes.

Greg stayed with him while George entered the room he'd seen the figure go into earlier. It was empty, so he checked under the bed and in the wardrobe, then went towards a built-in cupboard. He opened the door and stared down at a woman scrunched up in a ball on the floor, her face on her knees.

"Shawnee Wetherby?"

She didn't move.

"You need to come with us. We've got your nan."

She looked up at him and sighed, her eyes filling, and slowly stood. Then she darted towards him, her head down and whacking him in the stomach, but he stood his ground and didn't stumble backwards. He grabbed a fistful of her hair and held her steady with his other hand clamped around the top of her arm.

"Listen to me, you stupid fucking cow. We know what you've been up to, so there's no point fighting me. You're going to walk out of here nice and calmly or kicking and screaming, I couldn't give a monkey's which, but you *will* be coming with me."

She spat in his face.

"Of all the things you could have done to me, that's my least favourite form of retaliation. You're going to pay for that, sunshine."

He wiped the wetness on his shoulder, still keeping both hands on her, then he dragged her out of the room and into the hallway. "Watch her, she's a spitter."

Greg, who stood next to Eamon, shook his head. "Got any wet wipes, mate? My brother doesn't like people spitting on him."

"There's soap in the bathroom," Eamon said.

Greg went along the hall and through a doorway, coming back out with a wedge of wet tissue and a dollop of blue liquid soap on top.

"My left jaw." George let him clean the mess. He jerked Shawnee upwards so he could look her in the eye. "How are we playing this?"

"I'll come without a fight, but only because you said you've got my nan."

George let her go.

"Do you have someone who helps you out around the flat?" he asked Eamon.

"No, but the social worker comes, and so does the lady who checks my medicine."

"How often do they come?"

"The social lady comes on Mondays and the medicine lady is every Wednesday morning at ten o'clock, or sometimes it's three minutes past, it depends on the traffic lights."

"We're going to look into seeing if you can have some proper help and some company. Would you like that?"

"Like a nurse?"

"Sort of, but more like a friend. They can read to you or play board games, stuff like that, so we know you're safe and people like Shawnee and Andre can't take advantage." George gave her an evil glare.

"It won't be Fish and Chips, will it?"

"Um, no."

"Okay then."

"Someone will come and see you tomorrow, all right? We need to contact the social lady to ask if it's okay first. What's her name?"

"Miss Daulton."

"Brilliant. My brother will give you a card with a phone number on it. If you're worried or you feel unsafe, I want you to phone it or send a message."

"All right. Shall I send one now then, because I'm scared."

George stared at Shawnee. "Look at him. How could you use him like that?"

She didn't answer, although maybe she did — lowering her eyes could be taken as a sign of shame.

"No need to be scared," George told him. "We'll also give you a special phone, one you only use to talk to us, all right?"

"All right."

"We're going now."

George prepared himself for Shawnee to run as soon as they opened the front door. He sent a message to Carling to tell them to come round the front and get ready to catch her should she decide not to behave herself. Once two shapes appeared on the other side of the glass, George nodded to Greg who opened the door.

George held the top of Shawnee's arm again. "Little white van just there. I'm sure you saw it when we came to your house. The back door's open. Get in."

They trooped to the road. George spotted the kids he'd paid off. They loitered in the alleyway stuffing their faces with crisps and sweets. He caught their eye, lifted a finger to his lips to tell them to keep this quiet, and locked Shawnee in the back of the van. He gave Carling and Tez a wave to let them know their part in this was over, then he got in the passenger seat. He glanced over to where Eamon stood at the front door, fiddling with his fingers.

"Poor bastard," he said to Greg.

Chapter Twenty-Two

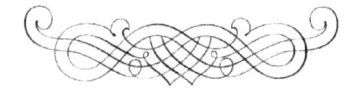

After a while of living inside the house with other women, Miranda had oddly got used to the way things worked. She found the routine a comfort now, but at first she'd wanted to baulk against it. She'd been warned not to a couple more times by Mocha before she'd finally accepted her fate. Or so it seemed. Like she had in Ward F, she could play the game so long as she

ended up getting what she wanted—which was freedom to go back to her old life and do the studies Bunty had suggested.

A lot of the time, when she was alone in the dormitory she shared with two other women, she cursed herself for changing her trajectory. She should have stuck with making the hundred thousand and moving on, but no, she'd fucked up by using some of the cash for the designer gear, then she'd had to make the money all over again to replace it, and then that stupid game where she'd played at being a sex worker on the street as if she knew what she was doing.

When those three women had gone missing one by one from the industrial estate, she should have given it up. She should have realised she wasn't as savvy as she'd imagined. How thick could she get? How naïve? How dumb had she been to continue to believe Mocha was a genuine customer even after the alarm bells had rung? She wasn't worldly wise, Val had pointed that out once, and Miranda agreed, but she'd learn to be in order to get out of here.

She often thought of her money in the safe at home and how she was so glad she'd told Bunty about it—and where it was. She trusted the woman who'd become a mother figure to her, and hopefully, if someone grassed Miranda up to the council for not living at her house, Bunty would go in and retrieve the safe before any moving company went in there.

She wished she could message her now to let her know she was all right. She was likely frantic with worry and imagining all sorts—funnily enough, like Miranda being abducted, except Bunty would probably think she'd been killed and left in a ditch somewhere, not incarcerated in a bloody nice house in the middle of nowhere.

But there was no way she could reach Bunty. Not yet anyway. Miranda's phone had been taken away from her by the man who'd come out of the house the night she'd been brought here. Julian, his name was. He clearly wasn't cut out for this kind of thing. He wasn't any good at pretending to be scary, although he gave it a good go from time to time. Mocha, on the other hand, could switch from one personality to another so fast it took her by surprise. He could sound mean as fuck.

She'd had the feeling ages ago they were supposed to be working as a team, Julian and Mocha, and not because they wanted to but because they had no choice. Mocha had outright told her that recently, and from the other things he'd said, she'd deduced that he wished he could be anywhere but here. Lucky for him, he was allowed to leave the house and drive wherever he wanted. He went to his mum's every Sunday for a roast dinner. For a few hours each day he could pretend everything was normal and that he didn't have to look after women who'd been kidnapped and forced to perform sex acts for no pay.

Apparently, they were supposed to be grateful to have a roof over their heads and food in their bellies. All their clothes had been bought for them, mainly loungewear for when they weren't working and weird floaty nightdresses, lacy lingerie, and high heels for when they were.

By now, after so many months here, she'd accepted she'd probably lost her house if Bunty had reported her missing, which she surely must have done. Would the council be so awful as to give her home to someone else while her whereabouts was unknown, though? Maybe she'd get lucky and escape, then she could go back as if she'd never left. Minus fucking about as a street worker. She didn't think about it much, though. Best not to when she had to concentrate on her behaviour here. One wrong step and it could be the end of the road for her.

Hopefully not. She'd quickly assessed the situation from the moment she'd stepped foot inside the house for the first time. Mocha acted tough in front of everyone, but she'd seen the vulnerability lurking underneath and made it her mission to exploit that. She had it in mind to pretend that being here wasn't a problem these days, that actually, she was grateful to be taken care of. Bullshit, but no one else needed to know. Candy, one of the women, was genuinely pleased to be here as her former life had been nothing to write home about, and even though they had to participate in weird rituals on top of huge stone beds in the middle of nowhere, Candy said it was better than what she'd had to go through before.

But what if that *was all an act, too?*

Tara, who didn't live here anymore, had never liked being in this house and she'd let everyone know about it often. She'd refused to have a working name, too, even though it meant Mocha had slapped her around the face for her defiance. But she wasn't a problem anymore, she was dead. She'd thrown herself out of the SUV while it had been driving along and had died after hitting the ground. Mocha had been looking for someone to take her place for quite a while, but he'd said the three industrial estate women were still in the news a lot so it meant people were being extra vigilant. He'd told her if he didn't find a new woman soon he'd be in deep trouble with his boss.

That would be the man calling himself the High Priest, someone who turned up at the rituals but never showed his face, hiding it behind a white plastic mask, the same as all the others who paid for the privilege of attending one of the creepy gatherings—the 'red disciples' in their scarlet cloaks and the 'watchers' in their black ones, all dancing to weird music and either participating in or observing sexual acts with the women who had to lie still and let them get on with it.

They'd been warned that if they didn't obey, Mocha and a few others had guns they wouldn't hesitate to use. Miranda had long since gathered that was just a threat. Mocha and Julian often talked business in front of the women. It was as if they were all one big happy family. Apparently, the High Priest charged a thousand pounds per customer, per night, for the rituals. The bloke must be loaded.

Miranda hadn't made the same mistake as Tara. She'd done as she was told and was known as Pearl now. No one needed to know that not only had she chosen it because of what pearls represented to her, but it was a reminder to herself that she had money waiting out there and a new life. She could reinvent herself. No longer the girl forced into the sex trade or the kid who'd tried to kill herself. No longer the vulnerable person on Ward F or the silly cow who'd stood on street corners, thinking she knew it all. She'd be none of those things anymore. If she made something of herself she could even move away, then nobody would know her past. The slate would be wiped clean.

She got up to make a cup of tea in the kitchen downstairs—there was also a kitchenette in the dormitory along with an en suite. Fantasy, the other woman, had gone out tonight with Julian and Mocha. A new recruit might be arriving. Unusually, Pearl and Candy had been left to roam the house instead of being locked in the dormitory until everyone else had arrived home. Mocha said earlier he trusted her not to try and escape now. They'd been having sex and sharing secrets for ages, and while it appeared on the surface she was complying, really she just bided her time until she could get the house keys off him and escape.

But that didn't mean she knew where to go once she left here. None of them had seen the outside of the house since the night they'd arrived, and as it had been dark, the distant surroundings had been hidden by the night's shadows. They all had to wear blindfolds when they travelled in a lorry to the locations where the stones were set up. How stupid she'd been to believe Mocha had a kink in wanting her to wear that blindfold when she'd got into the SUV. It was all a ruse to stop her from seeing where he was taking her.

She should have listened to those gut instincts a bit more.

God, once again she wished she could get hold of a phone and ring Bunty. But what was the point? With no location to give her, and some kind of blocker that stopped mobile phones being traced to this house (apparently), Pearl wouldn't be able to be rescued anyway.

But she wasn't giving up.
One day she'd get out of here.
It just wasn't today.

The new girl raised Pearl's hackles, especially because she'd already got pally-pally with Fantasy, which wasn't surprising. If Pearl had been kidnapped and another woman had already been in the car, she'd have bonded with her instantly, too.

Empress had been found at the industrial estate, standing there all by herself, a prime target for abduction. What a stupid fucking tart. That went for Mocha, too. He'd taken a huge risk in going back there. The police could have been nearby, watching, or a camera could have been set up. Regardless, he'd picked Empress up and brought her back here, and Pearl could only hope that coppers or journalists had *been hanging around there and had followed the SUV. Maybe they'd get saved any second.*

She sat up on her double bed and stared over at the newbie. They'd been contemplating what she should call herself. "You look like a bit of a princess to me." It was a spiteful jibe, as in Empress seemed high-maintenance, and Pearl felt bad, but she'd never say so. She was actually insecure, deep down—what if Mocha took a shine to the latest recruit and dropped her like a sack of shit? That would mean she couldn't get her hands on the keys.

"Empress," the newbie said.

"What happened? I'm Candy by the way."

"And I'm Pearl." God, could she sound any more desperate not to be left out? She recognised what was happening—she might well lose her Queen Bee status here, and panic was seeping in.

"Let her get her breath back for a minute," Fantasy said. "Then she can tell you."

"Are you from the same place as the others?" Candy asked, ignoring Fantasy's request. "Only, I think that's a bit dangerous going there, considering they've been abducted then murdered."

"Murdered?" Empress' eyes widened. "What the bloody hell's been happening here?"

Fucking hell, she's going to go off on one if we're not careful. I'm going to have to take control.

"Tell us about you first." Pearl went over and took Empress to a spare bed. "Get comfortable. Fantasy will get you a drink."

Fantasy stuck the kettle on without quibbling.

Empress told them about herself. No family or friends, no bloke, and a job as a sex worker that had landed her here. Then they discussed the rules, going on to inform Empress about the three industrial estate women being killed, then how Pearl, Fantasy, Candy, and Tara had been a foursome. Until Tara 'ran away' as Candy put it.

"Tara jumped out of a moving car," Pearl corrected her, "and it killed her."

Empress appeared horrified. "God, that's awful."

"It is." Candy plucked at her quilt cover. "So you can kind of see why we've decided to stay put and behave. I'd rather live here than be dead, and it's like I have a family now."

"I suppose," Empress said.

Pearl was going to have to watch her. She seemed trouble, and if it became clear she was going to fuck up Pearl's plans, then there'd be hell to pay.

Just like when she'd left Ward F behind, Miranda had settled into life outside that horrible house as though she'd never been away. Bunty had dealt with the council, and the home was safe.

The police hadn't widely broadcast the fact that Miranda had gone missing because Bunty hadn't told them she was a sex worker, so her disappearance hadn't been linked to the ladies from the industrial estate. Bunty had kept that quiet, worried Miranda would get in trouble with the DWP for claiming benefits while working cash in hand, and it wasn't until she'd discussed everything with Miranda afterwards that she'd worried she'd hampered any chances of her being found. Miranda had assured her that even if she'd told the police everything, she doubted very much it would have made a difference.

Miranda hadn't become the hero and found the keys to free everyone from the house. It had happened in a completely different way.

Men had turned up in balaclavas to rescue them.

She'd met up with Candy, Fantasy, and Empress recently in the French Café for a catch-up. Funny how she'd allowed herself to meet them but not Alicia and Val. Why was that? Alicia and Val had been good to her, but was it because being sectioned was linked to them in her mind and she didn't want to be reminded of it? Did that mean she was okay about being reminded of her time in the house? Probably. Like Candy, she'd found a family, people who actually gave a proper shit about her, something she'd never had while living with her mother. It had been a revelation to live with the women and talk deep into the night in the dormitory, a sisterhood of sorts, and then there was getting to know Mocha, who, according to Empress, seemed to have gone missing.

She wondered whether the balaclava men had something to do with that.

And who bloody knew Empress was an undercover copper?

It was over, but then Miranda had walked from the frying pan into the fire. Instead of studying, she'd fallen back on what she knew best and decided to return to sex work. She'd approached the leader of the Proust Estate where she lived to ask for a permit so she'd be allowed to tout for business. She hadn't expected Jet Proust to offer her a job as her right-hand woman.

Then life had got **really** *interesting.*

Chapter Twenty-Three

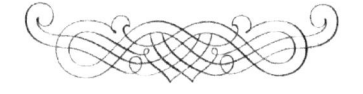

Once again, Pearl stood in the twins' warehouse, only this time the punchbag and its contents were nowhere to be seen, and in their place were two women. One of them was white, held still by chains hanging from the ceiling, and the other, young and black, had been manhandled into the building and down the stairs by George.

Jet and Pearl had come back out in the same wigs as earlier, although they'd both opted for more comfortable clothing now that they didn't have to appear to be posh Italians. Knowing they were coming to a grubby cellar had also been a good reason not to dress up.

"Ladies, meet Isla and Shawnee."

It was more than a little weird for George to make introductions as though this was nothing but a normal gathering, but Pearl was now used to this sarcastic type of behaviour because Jet behaved much the same way.

Am I strange for liking it?

"Isla and Shawnee, meet Jet Proust, leader of the Proust Estate, and Pearl, her right-hand woman, although I'm sure *you* know exactly who they are, don't you, Shawnee?"

Shawnee tried wrench her arm out of George's grip, but he held her too tightly. She pushed air out through clenched teeth and released a nasty growl. Then she switched her attention to Isla. "Are you okay, Nan? Have they been horrible to you?"

"This is the first time we've fucking met her," George said, "so how the fuck can we have hurt her?"

Isla appeared to be thinking deeply.

Shawnee frowned.

"This is the first time you've asked if I'm okay. Ever." Isla sighed. "It was always about you, even before your mum died. You never took into account that I'd lost my only daughter, and I accepted that because you were the most important one, you were young and had lost your mother, and I knew how that felt, but I do remember wondering when you'd ever ask me how I was."

"Nan? What the *fuck* has this got to do with the current situation?"

"Everything."

"You're not making sense."

"That bloke over there," George said. "His name's Moody. He went and collected your nan, and going by the fact she's got no bruises, I say he didn't have to hurt her."

"Why is she chained up?" Shawnee gestured to the manacles around Isla's wrists.

"Because I doubt very much that Moody fancied chasing her all around the fucking warehouse if she tried to run away, not that I've got to explain anything to you."

"Why's she here?"

"It was so we could have a chat with her, to get it out of her where you were."

"But she didn't know. I haven't seen her for days."

"We know that now, because a couple of canaries were singing in the Crown about where you were."

"That fucking Puggy."

"Who's that?" Jet asked.

"Going by the surname, it's a nickname for the kid who rents the flat she was in. Eamon Puggle." George stared at Shawnee. "What about him?"

"It had to be him who told Fish and Chips where I was, then Fish and Chips have gone and told someone, who then told you."

"We don't know if it was Fish and Chips who told our men, but someone did, and thanks to them, here we are."

"Who the *fuck* are Fish and Chips?" Jet asked, getting arsey.

George explained. "Although we don't know their real identities."

Shawnee said, "You don't need my nan. Let her go."

"It sounds to me like you think you can call the shots," George said, "and to be frank with you, it's pissing me off. No, we might well not need your nan anymore, but we do need to have a chat with her to see whether she can keep a secret. If she's anything like Puggy, who *can't* keep his gob shut, then she won't be leaving this cellar any other way than in bits through that trapdoor under her feet. But if she *can* keep a secret, which I think she can, considering she's been selling stolen goods from her house for the past twenty bastard years and hasn't ever parted with any protection money… The question is, would she still want to continue her money-making scheme on the quiet without us asking her for protection money, or would she rather go to the police and tell them that I've caved your fucking head in with a shovel?"

Isla glanced between George and her granddaughter. "What the hell did you do, Shawnee? Did you kill a man like he said?" She flashed a hand over towards Moody sitting in the corner, the chains jangling. She fixed her sights on Shawnee again. "I told him you'd never do that.

Yes, you'd steal, but I'd swear blind you'd never murder."

"I don't know what you're on about, Nan. He's been making shit up."

"So you didn't write all that stuff on your computer, like how you killed him with a pole and you put the poor fucker in a punchbag?"

Shawnee lowered her eyes.

Isla closed hers, but only for a moment. She levelled her gaze on Shawnee, her disappointment shining bright in her frown and the downturn of her mouth. "So you did then. I can't condone it, kid. I can't say it was okay to go that far just to get money. You should have nicked his drugs, transferred money from his account at the point you knew all his passcodes, but you never should have killed him. That was a step too far."

"I'm sorry," Shawnee said.

"Probably only sorry you got caught." Isla took a deep breath. "I love you, you know that, but you must also know that you're going to die today, and while I'll be grieving, while it's going to tear me up inside, I've still got to eat, I've still got to help all those people who I get the hooky gear for. That's why I agreed to talk to you for the twins, to make you confess, because *I* don't want to pay for what you've done. Call me a nasty old bitch, a traitor, but like I said, you're going to be dead no matter what I do. I'll always love you, but you've been such a stupid little cow…"

Pearl could understand what Isla was saying, she was being practical, but it wasn't pleasant to witness the pain in both women, one admitting she'd committed murder, the other admitting she was basically giving the twins her blessing to end her granddaughter's life as long as they set her free. It was bloody uncomfortable to be honest, a raw moment that should have happened in private. Maybe then they'd have hugged, cried, forgiven each other, but as it was, there were a couple of metres between them and no chance of a reconciliation happening anytime soon.

George kept hold of Shawnee while Greg unlocked Isla's manacles.

"So long as you don't breathe a word about this," George said to Isla, "we won't come round for protection money—or to give you a Cheshire."

Isla shook her head in fear. "Please, don't give me one of those. Everyone will know I've gone against you."

How odd that, rather than focusing on her granddaughter's imminent death, Isla had chosen to worry about whether her face would be cut from one side to the other. It gave Pearl a moment's pause. Her mother would have done the same. She'd have picked herself.

If Shawnee hadn't lowered her eyes, indicating she'd killed Andre, would Isla have chosen to stand by her no matter what? Or was Isla an inherently selfish person who'd always looked out for herself? Were she and Shawnee cut from the same cloth?

Whatever, the decision had been made, and Moody took Isla's arm, leading her up the stairs. How was she feeling at the sound of Shawnee screaming for her nan to 'fucking get back here and have the guts to watch me die, you old bitch'? Did her stomach clench? Was she crying? Did she wish she'd stayed in the cellar to hold Shawnee's hand when she died? Or was she taking the easy route so she wouldn't have to see or hear what was going to happen?

And why had George and Greg let her go? Did they think she'd be useful to them in the future? Jet had made similar decisions before, ones that didn't make sense to Pearl, but she supposed over time as leaders they'd grown to gauge who'd keep their mouth shut and who wouldn't, who was telling the truth and who wasn't, and who deserved to live and who didn't.

Maybe Isla was just some woman who sold stolen gear, nothing more, and Pearl hoped for the twins' sake that was the case.

She was brought out of her head by movement on a monitor on the wall at the bottom of the stairs. It showed a blindfolded Isla being led to a car and helped into the passenger side. Moody put her seat belt on her, then he got in and drove away. Pearl looked at Shawnee. She also watched the screen, in disbelief, shaking her head as if she couldn't believe her nan had walked out and left her to her fate.

"Were you good to her?" Pearl asked.

Shawnee stared at her. "What?"

"I said, were you good to her?"

"What are you on about?"

"Or did you treat her like shit and that's why she's left you to it? Have you given her a lifetime of grief and this is the last straw? Because we're all standing here, gobsmacked that a woman would leave her granddaughter like that, so there's got to be more to it. What the hell did you do to her to make her turn her back?"

"Exactly what I thought," Jet said.

Shawnee clamped her lips shut.

Pearl ignored her. Something had clicked inside her today. She'd found the place she belonged the most, in this insane world of gangs and violence, but where people righted the wrongs—undoubtedly in the wrong way sometimes, but they got the job done. Maybe she enjoyed helping the people who needed justice. Maybe this was finally her special place to roost, a nest she could stay in forever.

Chapter Twenty-Four

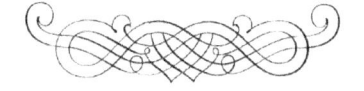

For the first time in her life, Shawnee was ashamed of how she'd treated her nan. They said karma was a bitch, and she understood the meaning of it now. So this was what it felt like to have no one left. She thought she'd felt like that when Mum had died, but she hadn't had a bloody clue. She'd still had Nan who'd tried her best to be a stand-in mother, but Shawnee had pushed her away. She should have been kinder. She should have taken all the hugs that were offered—and offered some back. She should have been more grateful to be wanted.

She allowed George to cuff her with the manacles which were still heated from Nan's skin. Shawnee had a last bit of warmth from her, at least. Nan would be giving her comfort and not even realise it. A bit like she had by Shawnee knowing she was just on the end of the phone. But Shawnee hadn't bothered to ring or text her much. Instead, she'd told herself to go it alone and only go round Nan's when she wanted something from her storage room, or she gave her a quick hug in the Crown, chatted for a few minutes to be polite, and then she'd gone her own way.

She'd been a bitch, and maybe she deserved this…whatever was going to happen to her.

Greg turned a handle on the wall. The chains clicked and tinkled, and she was raised from the floor, unable to touch it even when she pointed her toes downwards. She braced herself, because what was about to come was going to hurt. In what seriously felt like a dark and dreary dungeon, like the ones in her nightmares, Shawnee suffered the indignity of having her clothes cut away from her by the twins using Stanley knives. Greg put some of the material in a wood burner, closing the door but remaining where he stood, perhaps so he could feed more into the flames later. Was he just going to stand there doing that while George was the one who killed her? And what about Jet and Pearl? Would they join in or only watch?

They looked a ruthless group, their fists clenched, devoid of any expression that could let Shawnee know how they were feeling. Did they want to strike her? Did any of them have a twinge of sympathy for her? George approached, cocking his head and studying her, maybe poised to dart back in case she spat on him again. Then he beat her, merciless, the *thwack* of each blow echoing off the stone walls. She gritted her teeth against the onslaught of the pain his fists brought, refusing to give any of them the satisfaction of hearing her cry or scream or beg to be set free.

George kept on and on, his fists hitting her everywhere, and her strength waned. The blows to her face had produced a swollen eye that she could barely see out of, but when she looked down at her naked body, it was covered in bruises and blood. It was inevitable she was going to die, she'd known that from the minute George and Greg had turned up at Puggy's in disguise. She'd known it was them by their voices.

George's face was shiny with sweat, his fists covered in blood, his features twisted by his determination to kill her with his bare hands. Was that what he was trying to achieve here?

Another punch, and he split her top lip. She tasted blood and gathered it in her mouth, stared him at him with her one good eye, then spat at him.

Fuck you.

Chapter Twenty-Five

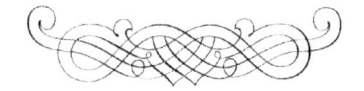

Blood dripped into her mouth from a lip so split that the cut reached halfway to her septum. George reckoned she was close to passing out, and a few well-placed whacks to her head would see her brain damaged. But he'd had enough now, and unless Jet wanted a go, he'd end it.

He turned to look at Jet, who nodded and walked over to the tool table.

"Hang on," Greg said to her. "Let me go up and get you a forensic suit."

George hadn't bothered with one. He'd been so fucking angry that Isla had felt the need to walk away from her granddaughter like that—not because Isla had done the wrong thing, but because something must have happened for her to make such a decision. You didn't just turn your back on family for no reason.

When Moody had brought her to the warehouse, he'd sent George a message warning him that she may well have to be silenced when all was said and done. George had asked why, and Moody said she'd admitted she'd lie for Shawnee. But when it had come down to the wire, or maybe because she'd had time to think about things while she'd been chained up, she'd chosen herself rather than Shawnee.

Maybe one day George would go round there for a cuppa to ask her why.

Greg returned with the suit, and Jet slipped it on over her outfit, handing her sunglasses to Pearl and then lifting her hood and tucking her hair away. Greg also gave her some gloves which she pulled on. She selected a knife with a blade of about ten inches and stood in front of Shawnee.

"What gave you and Scott the idea that he could come to my Estate and show me such a level of disrespect by impersonating someone else? This has been going on for *weeks* via phone calls. Did you think you'd get away with it? You must have done, otherwise he wouldn't have gone to the art gallery." She held the knife up. "Spill your guts to me before I do it for you. I'll disembowel you, no fucking problem. I've dealt with so many people like you, and like them, you're not as tough as you think."

"Fug you."

"Oh dear, having trouble speaking?" George asked.

"There's no more time left for games or lies, Shawnee," Jet said. "We all know why you're here, but if you need us to show you the evidence we've got that proves what you did, I'd be happy to. We could let you go, of course. Drop your naked self off at the police station, along with your laptop, and let them deal with you, but I don't want you to live, not after what you've done."

"Not only to Andre but to that poor sod in the flat," George said. "Using a vulnerable person for your own ends is disgusting."

"Do you have anything to say for yourself?" Jet asked. "Do you have any remorse for stealing a man's business and his life because you're too greedy to set up your own drug-dealing outfit? What makes you think it's okay to rob someone else's hard work and pretend it's your own?"

"She's scum," Greg said, feeding more clothing into the fire.

Jet stepped closer and lifted the blade to press it to one side of Shawnee's throat. She swiped to the right, the skin opening in a wide smile, blood spurting and gushing, drenching Shawnee's skin. The life drained out of the girl until she hung limp, then George gripped her ankles from behind, pulled her up backwards, and Greg used a hook on a pole to open the trapdoor.

Using the sleeve of her suit, Jet wiped the blood from her face and stepped back to stand beside Pearl. "Are you okay?"

"Yeah."

"No regrets?"

"No, I've found home."

"With me or with them?"

"With all of you."

George smiled at that, and he whistled throughout cutting Shawnee into pieces and letting the bits plop into the water. It had been a bloody long day, but once they were all showered, he'd suggest going to the Taj for dinner. He could just do with a biryani.

Chapter Twenty-Six

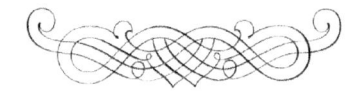

A long time had passed since Puggy had met The Brothers. As promised, someone had turned up the next day to talk about playing board games and stuff. John had been nice enough, but Puggy had let George know that he didn't feel comfortable enough to have someone in his flat as often as John had suggested visiting.

Maybe he was cutting off his nose to spite his face, because he didn't have any friends and he really missed the people coming round to buy the baggies, but there was something about John that bothered him. A bit pushy, and he asked a lot of questions.

Puggy didn't like answering questions unless it was Miss Daulton asking them.

Someone had indeed come round to put the shoe cupboard together and hand him a burner phone, and since Shawnee had cleaned the flat so well, Puggy had been able to keep on top of it much better. She'd given him tips on how to stop himself from becoming overwhelmed with the housework, and now he got up every day and made his bed, made sure the washing was on, and tidied up as he went along.

He had physio later, but it was his last session, seeing as he'd started going out for walks instead of sitting in his chair all the time. Life was looking up, especially because Miss Daulton was arranging for him to go to the community centre to make new friends. He was waiting for her to let him know whether he'd got a place in three of the classes. She'd said they were neurodivergent groups and perfect for him. She was on a mission to help him have a better life.

The doorbell rang, and he frowned. He hadn't ordered a pizza or anything, and it wasn't Monday so Miss Daulton wasn't due, and anyway, she always messaged to ask if it was okay if she needed to pop round on any other day. It wasn't Wednesday either, or ten a.m., so Mrs Kapor, the medicine lady, wouldn't be at the door either.

He wiped some dribble from his bottom lip and went into the kitchen to look outside and see who was there. He gasped and jumped back, wanting to pull the blind down so he could hide. Fish and Chips were there. What did they want? He was scared, so did that mean he should phone the twins? If he did, and he said Fish and Chips were bad men, they'd post fifty quid through his letterbox when it got dark, like they had before when he'd told them stuff that was going on out the front.

"Oi, Puggy," Fish said through the letterbox. "Do you fancy another job to earn some more pocket money?"

Puggy loved pocket money, it meant he could buy all the things he liked. His benefits didn't pay him enough to do what he wanted, and he'd struggled with his finances since Andre had stopped needing him.

He shuffled out into the hallway and looked at the eyes in the letterbox slot—eyes surrounded by the creepy black wool of a balaclava. "How much pocket money?"

"Loads."

"And what's the job?"

"We'd best come in to talk about that—because it's a secret."

To be continued in *Raffia*,
The Cardigan Estate 41

Printed in Great Britain
by Amazon